NOT NOT
WHILE THE GIRO

James Kelman was born in Glasgow in 1946.
His books include *The Busconductor Hines*, *A
Chancer* and *Greyhound For Breakfast*, which
won the 1987 Cheltenham Prize and a Scottish
Arts Council Book Award. His novel, *A Disaffection*
was published earlier this year. *Not Not While
the Giro* also won a Scottish Arts Council Book
Award in 1983. James Kelman lives in Glasgow
with his wife and two daughters.

By the same author

An Old Pub Near the Angel
and other stories
Three Glasgow Writers
(with Tom Leonard and Alex Hamilton)
Short Tales from the Night Shift
The Busconductor Hines
Lean Tales
(with Agnes Owens and Alasdair Gray)
A Chancer
Greyhound for Breakfast
A Disaffection

JAMES KELMAN

NOT NOT
WHILE THE GIRO
AND OTHER STORIES

Minerva

A Minerva Paperback

NOT NOT WHILE THE GIRO

First published 1983
by Polygon Books
This Minerva edition published 1989
by Mandarin Paperbacks
an imprint of Reed Consumer Books Limited
Michelin House, 81 Fulham Road, London SW3 6RB
and Auckland, Melbourne, Singapore and Toronto

Reprinted 1990, 1991, 1993

British Library Cataloguing in Publication Data
Kelman, James
  Not not while the giro : and other stories.
  I. Title
  823'.914[F]

  ISBN 0-7493-9028-X

The Publisher acknowledges subsidy from Scottish Arts Council
towards the publication of this volume.

Excerpt from *Breathe deep and regular with it*
by kind permission of the author

Printed and bound in Great Britain by
Cox & Wyman Ltd, Reading

for Marie

Contents

He knew him well

The old man lowered the glass from his lips and began rolling another cigarette. His eyes never strayed until finally he lit up, inhaling deeply. He stared at me for perhaps thirty seconds then cleared his throat and began speaking. 'Funny places — pubs. Drank in here for near enough twenty years.' He paused, shaking his head slowly. 'Never did get to know him. No. Never really spoke to him apart from Evening Dennis, Night Dennis. Been in the navy. Yeh, been in the navy alright. Torpedoed I hear. 1944.' He paused again to relight the dead cigarette. 'One of the only survivors too. Never said much about it. Don't blame him though.' He looked up quickly then peered round the pub. 'No, don't blame him. Talk too much in this place already they do. Never bloody stop, it's no good.' He finished the remainder of his drink and looked over to the bar, catching the barman's eye who nodded, opened a Guinness and sent it across.

'Slate,' said the old guy, 'pay him pension day.' He smiled, 'Not supposed to drink this, says it's bad for me gut — the doctor.'

'Yeh?'

'Oh yeh.' He nodded. 'Yeh, said it would kill me if I weren't careful.' He was looking at me over the tops of his spectacles. 'Seventy two I am, know that? Kill me! Ha! Bloody idiot.'

'Did you like old Dennis though?' I asked.

'Well never really knew him did I? I would've though. Yeh, I would've liked old Dennis if we'd spoke. But we never talked much, him and me. Not really.' He paused for a sip of the beer, continued, 'Knew his brother of course — a couple of years older than Dennis I think. And a real villain he was. Had a nice wife. I used to work the racetracks then and sometimes met him down there.' The old man stopped again, carefully extracting the long dead roll-up from between his lips and putting it into his waistcoat pocket. He took out his tobacco pouch and rolled another. 'Yeh, Dennis' brother.' He lit the cigarette. 'He was a villain. He used to tell me a few things. Yeh, he made a living alright. Never came in here except to see old Dennis.'

'How did they get on together, okay?'

'What was that? Well . . .' He scratched his head. 'Don't really know. Didn't speak much to each other — some brothers don't you know.' He was looking over the glasses at me. 'No, they'd usually just sit drinking, sometimes laughing. Not speaking though. Not much anyhow, probably said everything I suppose. Course, maybe old Dennis would ask after his wife and kids or something like that.'

'Was he never married himself then?'

'Maybe. I don't rightly know. Guvnor'd tell you.'

'Who, him?' I pointed at the barman.

'What. Him! Ha.' The old guy snorted into his drink. 'Guvnor! He would like that. Bloody guvnor. No, his brother-in-law, Jackie Moore, he's the guvnor. But he's been laid up now for nearly a year. Broke his leg and it's never healed proper, not proper. Him!' He gestured at the barman. 'Slag thinks he'll get this place if Jackie has to pack it in . . .' The old guy's voice was beginning to rise in his excitement. 'No chance, no bleeding chance. Even his sister hates his guts.'

He was speaking too loudly now and I glanced across to see if the barman was loitering, but he seemed engrossed in wiping the counter. The old guy noticed my concern and he leaned over the table. 'Don't pay no attention,' He spoke quietly. 'He hears me alright. Won't let on though. Bloody ponce. What was I saying though — old Dennis, yeh, he could drink. Scotch he liked, drank it all the time. Don't care much for it myself. A drop of rum now and then, yeh, that does me.' He paused to puff on the cigarette, but had to relight it eventually. 'Used to

play football you know, old Dennis. Palace I think or maybe
the Orient. Course he was getting on a bit when the war went
on. Just about ready to pack it in. And he never went back
after.'

'Cause of his arm?'

'Yeh, the torpedo.' The old man was silent for several
moments, puffing on the roll-up between sips at the black rum
I'd got him. 'Funny he should've waited so long to do it. Nearly
as bleeding old as me he was! Course, maybe the arm had
something to do with it. Maybe not.' He scratched his head.
'Talk in this place they do. Wouldn't if Jackie was here. No, not
bloody likely they wouldn't.' He sucked on his teeth. 'No, not if
Jackie was here behind the bar.' He inhaled very deeply before
looking at me over the glasses. 'Where d'you find him then . . . I
mean what like was he when.' He stopped and swallowed the
last of the rum.

'Well, just like it said in the paper. I was a bit worried cause I
hadn't seen him for a couple of days so I went up the stair and
banged his door. No answer, so off I went to the library to see if
I could see him there.'

'The library?'

'Yeh, he used to go up before opening time, nearly every
day.'

'Yeh, expect he would,' said the old man, 'now I think on it.'

'Anyway,' I continued, 'I got home about half five and saw
the landlord's daughter. She was worried so I said did she want
me to force open the door or what, before her dad came back —
should I wait maybe. She said to do what I thought so I went
ahead and broke it in, and he was lying there, on the bed. The
wrist sliced open.'

'Yeh . . .' The old guy nodded after a moment, then added,
'And the eating, it said in the paper . . .'

'That's right. The doctor, he said old Dennis couldn't have
been eating for nearly a week beforehand.'

'Bloody fool,' he sighed. 'He should've ate. That's one thing
you should do is eat. I take something every day, yeh, make
sure of that. You got to. A drop of soup's good you know.'

I ordered two more drinks just on the first bell, we stayed silent, smoking then drinking, until I finished and rose and said, 'Well, I'm off. See you again.'

'Yeh,' he muttered, staring into his glass. He shook his head, 'Old Dennis should've ate eh!'

An old pub near the Angel

Charles wakened at 9.30 a.m. and wasted no time in dressing. Good God it's about time for spring surely. Colder than it was yesterday though and I'll have to wash and shave today. Must. The face has yellow lines. I can't wear socks either. Impossibility. People notice smells though they say nothing.

Think I will do a moonlight tonight, I mean five weeks rent — he has cause for complaint. Humanity. A touch of humanity is required. He has fourteen tenants paying around £3.00 each for those poxy wee rooms, surely he can afford to let me off paying once in a while. Man I've even been known to clean my room on occasion with no thought of rent reduction.

Still he did take me for a meal last night. Collapsed if he hadn't. Imagine that bloody hotel porter knocking me back from their staff canteen. Where's your uniform? Are you a washer-up? These people people depress me. What's the difference, one meal more or less. You'd think they were paying for the actual grub themselves. Old Ahmed though — what can I say — after the bollicking he gives me for not even trying to get a job and some bread together, who expects him to come back half an hour later saying, 'Okay you Scotch dosser, come and eat.' No, nothing to be said apart from, 'Fancy a pint first Ahmed?' Yes, he has too many good points. Suppose I could give him a week's money. Depends on what they give me though. Anyway.

Charles left the house and made his way towards the Labour Exchange up near Pentonville Road. It was a twenty five minute walk but one he didn't mind at all as he normally

13

received six and a half quid for his trouble, later on, from the
N.A.B.

Yes, spring is definitely around the corner man. Look at that
brief-case with the sports' jacket and cavalry twills. Already.
Very daring. Must be a traveller. Best part of the day this —
seeing all the workers, office and site and the new middle class
tradesmen, yes, all going about their business. It pleases me.

Can't say I'm in the mood for long waits though. Jesus Christ I
forgot a book. Man man what do I do now? Borrow newspapers? Stare at people's necks and make goo goos at their
children. Good God! the money's going to be well earned today.

Charles stopped outside the Easy Eats Cafe and breathed in
deeply. This fellow must be the best cook in London, without
any doubt at all. My my my. Everytime I pass this place it's the
same, smells like bacon and eggs and succulent sausages with
toast and tea. Never mind never mind soon be there.

Charles arrived at the Labour Exchange and entered door C
to take up position in the queue under D.

Well, I can imagine it this morning, 'Yes Mr. Donald there is
some back money owing to you. Would you sign here for
£43.68?' I'd smile politely, 'Oh yes thank you, I had been
beginning to wonder if it'd ever come through. Yes. Thank you.
Good day.' Then I'd creep out the door and run like the
clappers before they discovered the error. God love us! What's
this? Can't be somebody farting in a Labour Exchange surely!
Bloody Irish, don't understand them at all. Think they delight
in embarrassing the English just. Everybody kids on they didn't
hear. But surely they can smell it?

Charles stepped out the queue and tapped the culprit on the
shoulder. 'Hey Mick that's a hell of a smell to make in a public
place you know.'

'Ah bejasus,' he sighed, 'it's that bloody Guinness Jock. Sure
I can't help it at all.'

'Terrible stuff for the guts right enough.'

'Ah but it's better than that English water they sell here.
Bitter!' He shook his head, 'It's a penance to drink it
altogether.'

'Aye. You been waiting long?'

'Not at all.' He shook his head again and spat on the floor, wiping it dry beneath his boot. 'Want a smoke?'

'You kidding?'

'What you going on about. Here.' He took out a packet of Woodies and passed it to Charles. 'Take a couple Jock — I've plenty there and I'll be getting a few bob this morning.'

Charles accepted, sticking one behind his ear. He said, 'You been over long?'

'Ah too long Jock, too long.' He gave a short laugh. 'Still skint.' He struck a match off the floor and they lighted the cigarettes. 'Aye, if I'd been buying that Guinness in shares instead of pints I'd be worth a fortune and that's a fact — the hell with it.'

'Heh, you're next Mick.'

The Irishman went to the counter and received the signing-on card from the young girl clerk. He signed and was handed his pay slip then he walked over to the cashier where he was soon receiving the money, and he vanished. Charles followed the man who was next in line and was astonished to receive a pay slip. Normally he got a B1 form for the N.A.B. He asked the girl whether he would still be getting it. She smiled, 'Not this week anyway Mr. Donald.'

Charles strode to the money counter and stole a quick look at the pay slip. Good God! He looked again. He studied it. 'God love us,' he said loudly.

£23.82. Jesus. Oh you good thing. Nearly twenty four quid. Man man that must be near eighteen back pay! What can one say God? Mere words are useless.

He passed the slip under the grill to the older woman with the fancy spectacles. Once he had signed at the right place she counted and passed him the bundle of notes and coins.

'My sincere thanks madam,' he said.

The cashier smiled, 'That makes a change.'

'You have a wonderful smile,' continued Charles folding the wad. 'I shall certainly call back here again. Good morning.'

'Good morning.' The cashier watched him back off towards the exit.

He closed the door. Yes, maybe chances there if I followed it through. A bit old right enough. Maybe she just pities me. With that smile she gave me! Impossible.

He walked up Pentonville Road and decided to go for a pint rather than a breakfast. Half past eleven. Not too early.

'Pint of bitter and eh — give me . . .' Charles stared at the miserable gantry, 'just give me one of your good whiskies eh!'

The ancient bartender peered at him for a moment then bent down behind the bar to produce a dusty bottle of Dimple Haig. 'How's this eh?'

'Aye,' replied Charles, 'that's fine. How much is it?'

'Seven bob,' muttered the bartender rubbing his ear thoughtfully.

'Well give me twenty Players as well and that's that.'

The bartender passed over the cigarettes and grabbed the pound note, mumbling to himself. Very friendly old bastard. Must hate Scotsmen or something. He brought back the change and moved around the counter tidying up. 'Hoy!' called Charles after a time. 'Any grub?'

'What's that?' cried the bartender, left hand at his ear.

'Food, have you any food?'

'What d'you want, eh?'

'Depends. What've you got?'

'Don't know.' He thought for a moment, 'Potato crisps?'

'No chance,' said Charles. 'Is that it?'

'Shepherd's pie? The missus makes it,' he added with a strange smile.

Wonder why he's smiling like that. Poisoned or something?

'Homemade eh . . .' Charles nodded, 'Aye, I'll have some of that.'

'Now?'

'Yes, now for heaven sake.' He shook his head.

'Okay okay, just take a seat a minute, I'll go and tell her eh?' He shuffled away. As he passed through the door in the partition he glanced back at Charles who gave him a wave.

Kind of quiet place this. Wonder when it gets busy. Strange I'm the only customer at nearly twelve o'clock on a Thursday morning. The ancient bartender returned and cried, 'Bout ten fifteen minutes eh?' Charles nodded. The other resumed wiping some glasses.

Man man who would've thought of me getting paid back money like that. Brilliant. Let me see. 11.50 a.m. By rights I should still be sitting in the second interview queue at the N.A.B. The fat woman's kids'll be rolling on the floor and she'll be reading the *Evening Standard* dog-section. Yes, I'll be missed. They'll think I've gone to Scotland. Or maybe been lifted by the busies. No, won't have to go back there for a while. Thank Christ for that.

A huge woman appeared from behind the partition holding a great plateful of steaming shepherd's pie. 'One shepherd's pie!' she shouted. Her chins trembled and her breasts rested on her knees as she bent to plonk it down in the centre of Charles' table.

'This looks wonderful,' he said, sniffing at it. He smiled up at her. 'Madam, you've excelled yourself. How much do you ask for this delicious fare?'

'14 p.' She pointed to her husband. 'He'll give you the condiments. Just shout, he's deaf occasionally.'

'Many thanks,' replied Charles, placing thirty pence on her tray. 'Please have a drink on me.'

'Ta son,' she said and toddled back through to the kitchen.

Charles ate rapidly. He thoroughly enjoyed the meal. 'Hoy!' he called, 'Hoy!'

The bartender was standing, elbows propped on the counter, staring up at the blank television screen. 'Hoy!' shouted Charles getting out of his seat. He walked to the bar.

'Yeh yeh, yeh! What's up eh?'

'Another pint of bitter. And have one yourself.'

'What's that?'

'Jesus what's up here at all. Listen man get me a pint of bitter please and have one with me, eh! How's that. Eh?'

'Fine son, I'll have a half. Nice weather eh . . .' The ancient fellow was showing distinct signs of energy while pulling the beer taps. 'Pity about the Fulham though eh! Yeh, they'll be back, they'll be back.' He took a lengthy swig at his half pint, eyes closed, a slow stream trickling down his partly shaven chin and winding its way round the Adam's Apple on down beneath his frayed shirt collar. 'Yeh,' he said, 'Poor old Chelsea.' And he finished the rest of the drink.

'What about the old Jags though eh? I mean that's even worse than the Fulham surely!'

'What's that Jock?'

'The Thistle man, the old Partick Thistle, they were relegated last season.'

'Ah, Scotch team eh! Don't pay much heed.'

'Yeh, you're right and all. Not much good up there.'

'Bloody Celtic and Rangers,' he shook his head in disgust. 'Get them in here sometimes. And the bloody Irish. Mostly go down Kings Cross they do. Bloody trouble they cause eh?'

'Give us another of these Dimples.'

'Yeh,' He smiled awkwardly, 'Like them do you?' He pursed his lips.

Charles got it and returned to his table near the wall, and sat quietly for about five minutes. 'Hoy!' he shouted.

The bartender had regained his former position beneath the television set. He gave no indication of having heard.

'HOY!'

The old fellow jumped and turned angrily. 'What's up then? What's this bleeding hoy all the time eh?'

'Well you're a bit deaf for Christ sake.'

'No need to bloody scream like that though.'

'Alright alright, sorry. Look, I'm just going to go out for a paper a minute. Keep your eye on my drink eh?'

The bartender began muttering then started to polish glasses.

Charles had to visit three newsagents before obtaining a copy of the *Sporting Life*. Nothing else could possibly do with all that back money lying about. When he returned to the pub he noticed another customer sitting at a table facing him, just at the corner of the room. She was around ninety years of age.

'Morning,' called Charles. 'Good morning missus.'

The old lady was sucking her gums and smiled across at him, then she looked up at the bartender. 'Goshtorafokelch,' she said.

The bartender looked from her to Charles and back again before replying, 'Yeh, I'll say eh?'

Bejasus thank God I've got a paper to read. This must be an old folk's home in disguise. He quickly swallowed the remains of the whisky and then the remains of the beer. 'Hoy!' he shouted. 'What time is it? I mean is that the right time there or what?'

He frowned and then said, 'Must be after twelve I reckon eh?'

Charles got up and carried the empties across. 'Think I'll be going,' he said.

'You please yourself,' he muttered. 'Going to another shop are you eh?'

'No, it's not that man, I've just got to go home, get a bath and that.'

'Will you be back then eh?'

'Well, not today. Maybe tonight though, but if not I'll definitely be back sometime.'

'Ah — who cares eh?' The bartender poured himself a gin then said, 'Want a short do you eh?'

'WHAT?'

'Another short, one of them.' He pointed at the dusty Dimple Haig. 'Bleeding thing's been there for years,' he said and poured a fair sized measure out. 'Yeh, glad to get rid of it eh?'

Charles took the tumbler and looked at it. The bartender watched him drink some and asked, 'You really like it then eh Jock?'

'Aye, it's a good whisky.'

The barman opened a bottle of sweet stout and pushed it across to him. 'You pass that down to her,' he said.

'Right you are.' Charles walked over to the corner and put it down next to the old woman's glass. 'Here you are missus, the landlord sent it.'

She looked up and glanced at him with a smile and a nod of the head. 'Patsorpooter,' was what she said.

'Aye,' Charles grinned. 'Fine.' He went back to the bar to finish the whisky. 'Okay then,' he said, 'that's me, I'll be off. And I'll be back in again, don't worry about that.'

'Hm.' The bartender polished the counter. He moved on to another part of it.

'Listen,' called Charles, 'I'll be back.'

The ancient fellow was now polishing a large glass and seemed unable to hear for the noise of the cloth on it.

'I'll see yous later!' shouted Charles hopelessly.

He collected the newspaper and cigarettes from the table and made for the door. Christ this is really terrible. Can't understand what it's all about. Maybe . . . No, I haven't a clue. Sooner I'm out the better.

He stopped at where the old lady was sitting. 'Cheerio missus, I'll be in next week sometime. Okay?'

She wiped a speck of foam from the tip of her nose. 'Deef!' she cried, 'deef.' And she burst into laughter. Charles had a quick look round for the bartender but he must have gone through the partition door, so he left immediately.

Ten guitars

They stopped outside the gates to the Nurses' Home. He could see the night-porter peering through the window trying to identify the girl. The rain pattered relentlessly but not too heavily, down on her umbrella. 'I better go in,' she said, with a half smile, staring in at the little porter's lodge.

'Thought you were allowed till twelve before the gates were shut?' he asked.

She shrugged without replying and, shuffling her feet, began humming a song to herself.

'Come on we'll walk up the road a bit where there are no spies.'

'Oh Danny doesn't bother.' She had stepped backwards into the shadows, expecting him to follow. The night-porter turned the page of a newspaper with his left hand; he held a tea cup against his cheek with the other. Perhaps she was right. He didn't appear the least bit interested.

'Fancy a coffee?'

'In your flat I suppose!' she smiled.

'Well it's only a room, but it's warm, and I've got a chair.'

'That's not what I mean.'

He turned his coat collar up before answering. 'Listen, if you know any cafes still open we'll go there.' He could not be bothered. What he did want to say was listen, why don't you go in or why don't you come out, I'm getting tired and really, what's the diff anyway? But she was always having to play little games all the time.

'I'm only kidding,' she said.

'Yeh,' he smiled. 'Sorry. Come on then, let's go and drink coffee, I'm too tired to rape you anyway.'

'Very funny!' she laughed briefly.

He had met her at the hospital dance four weeks ago and this was the sixth time they had been out together. Cinema twice. Pub thrice. This evening she hadn't finished until 8 o'clock so they had dined in an Indian restaurant, had a couple of drinks afterwards and strolled back in the rain. He didn't find her tremendously attractive but she seemed to quite like him. They had had no sex yet. At the beginning he had attempted to get it going but this was waning and now amounted to little more than jokes and funny remarks on the subject. She was half a head shorter than him, dressed quite well if 6 months behind in style, had short black hair and wore this brown corduroy coat he liked the first times but not so much now. She had a sharp wee upturned nose, was nineteen years old, kissed with sealed lips and came from Bristol.

'No females allowed in here you know!' he said, quietly turning the key in the lock of the outside door. 'Under any circumstances.'

She giggled, gazing up and down the street. 'I can only stay ten minutes,' she whispered, peering into the gloomy and musty smelling hallway.

Beckoning her to follow they crept upstairs without switching on any lights. This place was known as a respectable bachelors-only house. It was wholly maintained by an eighty eight year old Italian lady who preferred older, retired if possible, gentlemen. She had only allowed him in through her husband whom he had met playing dominoes in the local pub. 'Steady boy,' he told his wife. But it was clean and quiet and during the short while he had been staying he had only twice set eyes on another tenant. On another occasion, just after closing-time, somebody had bumped against his door and seemed to fall upstairs. When he investigated whoever it was had vanished. He had concluded that the person was living directly above but could not be sure. The rent was £3.50 a week for this medium sized room containing a mighty bed which resembled his idea of what an orthopaedic bed must look like. It was shaped like a small but steep hill; four feet high at the top and half that at the bottom. Occasionally he woke up with his feet sticking out over the end and his head about eighteen inches below the pillows. An unusual continental quilt covered it all. The interior of the mattress seemed to be stuffed with potato crisp packets and startling crinkling noises escaped whenever he turned onto his side. It was extremely comfortable! Although there was no running water there was an old marble-topped table of some kind and an enormous jug and basin; underneath the table stood an enamel bucket, and all three vessels plus the battered electric kettle were filled daily with fresh water. There were no cooking facilities. Under no circumstances was cooking allowed in the house, even if he had gone out and bought his own cooker. The landlady was totally opposed to it. At first he would buy things like cheese and cold meat but recently he had discovered tinned frankfurters and boiled eggs. He emptied the frankfurters into the electric kettle and also one or two eggs. Once the water had boiled for three minutes the grub was ready for eating. The only snag was the actual kettle which was a very old model, it had a tiny spout and a really wee opening on top, maybe less than three inches in diameter. This meant he had to spear the frankfurters out individually with a fork which required skill, frequently leaving bits of sausage floating about after; and often the eggs would crack when dropped down onto the kettle bottom which caused the water to become cobwebby from the escaping egg white. Fortunately the flavour of the coffee never seemed all that impaired. He was secretly proud of his ingenuity but was unable to display it to the girl having neither frankfurter nor egg. Still, she did seem pleased to get the chair and the coffee. He switched on the gas-fire.

'Very quiet,' she said presently.

'Haunted.'

She smiled her disbelief.

'You don't believe me? There's things go bump in the night here, I'm telling you.'

'I don't believe you.'

'Okay . . .' Sitting on the carpet he began twiddling the knobs on the transistor radio. 'What's Luxembourg again?'

'208 metres. If I believed everything you told me I'd go mad or something.'

'Doesn't bother me if you're too nervous to hear.' He switched off the radio and continued in a low growling kind of stage-voice. 'One dark winter's evening just after closing time around the turn of the century, an aged retired navvy was returning home from the boozer . . .'

'Retired what?'

'Navvy. And he was still wearing his Wellingtons, returning from the boozer quietly singing this shanty to himself when he opened the front door and climbed the creaky stairs.' He paused and pointed at the door. 'Just as he passed that very door on his way up he stopped in terror, at the top he saw this death's head staring down at him. Well he staggered back letting out this blood curdling scream and went toppling down the stairs banging on that door as he went to his doom.'

'Did he?' she said politely.

'Yeh, really! They say to this day if you climb the stair occasionally just after closing-time you'll sometimes see a death's head wearing a pair of Wellington boots. I know it's hard to believe but there you are.'

She gazed above his head.

'Too much bloody interference at this time of night,' he muttered, back with the transistor radio. 'You want Radio 1?'

'There's nothing on after seven. I don't really mind.' She had begun humming this tune again to herself. Why the hell didn't she go! Sitting there like Raquel Welch. Anyway if she really did fancy him surely she'd want to kip up with him — at least for the night. Good Christ. And it was nearly 12 o'clock probably. Still, he didn't have to get up for work in the morning. But what would happen if they locked her out or something? Get chucked out the nurses' home? And he would get chucked out this place if Arrivederchi Roma found out.

'Want another coffee?'

'I don't mind.'

'Well yes or no?'

'If you're having one.'

'I'm not having one but if you want one just go ahead and say so.'

'I'm not fussy.'

Jesus why didn't she get up and go? 'Plenty of books there if you want a read . . .' He gestured vaguely beneath the bed where a pile of paperbacks was lying.

'No thanks.'

He ripped a piece of newspaper and stuck it through the grill of the gas-fire to get a light for his cigarette, and said, 'Did you never smoke?'

'Yes, quite heavily, but I gave it up last Christmas.'

'Mmm, good for you. I sometimes . . .' He lacked the energy to finish the sentence.

'There's jobs going in the hospital for storemen and porters,' she said.

'Is that right?'

'Yes, and they're earning good wages. The man you see is a Mister Harvey. They're desperate for staff.'

Perhaps she was only seeing him in an attempt to recruit him for the position of porter. She had begun humming that song again. He looked at her. 'What tune's that again?'

'Ten guitars. I've always liked it. It was only a B side. My big sister had it.'

Wish to Christ she was here just now. 'No,' he said, 'I like the fast numbers myself.'

'You would,' she laughed. She actually laughed! What was this? A note of encouragement at long last. What was he supposed to do now? He had not that much desire to start playing around again, too bad on the nerves. Anyway, she didn't have the brains to drop hints. She didn't even have the brains to . . .

'What was that?' she cried.

'What?'

'That noise.' She stared at the door.

'Ssh. Might be that old one creeping about, checking up on everybody. If she finds you here I'm right in trouble.'

'Oh,' she replied, relieved.

'You didn't believe that death's head twaddle did you!'

'Of course not — I'm used to you by now.'

What did she mean by that? He stood to his feet and walked to the cupboard to get the alarm clock. He began to wind it up. After setting it down again he stared at the back of her shoulders as she stared at the gas-fire, humming that song to herself. He had to try once more. It was getting ridiculous. Stepping over to her chair he kissed the nape of her neck. She did not move. Her blouse fastened at the back and he unbuttoned the top buttons and fumbled at the hook on her bra.

'What d'you think you're playing at?' she asked.

'Nothing. I'm taking off your blouse, but I'm stuck.' Then he discovered the catch thing and added, 'No I'm not.' He continued on the blouse again and she allowed it to slide off her shoulders and then folded it up and placed it neatly on the carpet. Meanwhile he held both strap ends of the bra. But he had reached this point before in the alley behind the hospital, and on the very first night after the dance he had managed to get his fingertips beneath the rim of her pants. What had been going wrong since? He stepped round the chair to face her. He took both her hands and pulled her to her feet and kissed her. Still unsure but almost letting himself believe this could only be it. Then he paused. She unzipped her skirt at the side and walked out of it, and climbed onto the bed and under the quilt. She reached back and slung the bra over the back of the bed.

'Never seen one of these before,' she said, indicating the quilt and unaware of his incredulous stare.

'It's a continental quilt!' he answered at last. He was still dazed when he undressed, down to his socks and underpants. He went to switch off the light. She giggled.

'What's up?'

'You! in your socks and skinny legs.' She laughed again, a bit shrilly.

'Lucky it's not a pair of Wellingtons!' he grinned, nervously, and marched forward.

But he had forgotten to alter the usual going-off time on the alarm clock and it burst out at ten a.m. as normal. Recognising the severity of the situation he jumped out of bed at once and dressed rapidly. The landlady rose at dawn and would have cleaned and exorcised the rest of the house by this time. Fortunately she wouldn't come into the room unless the door was open which he had to do first thing upon leaving every day. He told her to hurry up. What a confrontation if the old one burst through the door! 'Come on,' he whispered.

She found her pants among the fankle of sheets and quilt at the foot of the bed and quickly slipped them on. Attempting to pull up her tights she toppled onto the bed and giggled.

'Ssh for Christ sake — she's got ears like a fucking elephant.'

'No need to swear.'

'Sorry, but you better hurry.'

When finally she was ready he went out and then she did, and he closed the door gently. He looked upstairs and downstairs but no sign of the old one. Maybe out shopping or something! He was now standing on the first landing before the hallway. She came behind, clutching her coat and handbag. 'Got everything?' he asked.

She nodded, unable to speak.

He walked quickly and opened the outside door and peered up the street and down the street. No one! Grabbing her by the hand he tugged her down the seven steps to the pavement and they strode along the street in the direction opposite the one usually taken by the landlady.

Shortly after midday he returned. They had eaten breakfast then she had gone to get ready for duty, against his wishes. She always took her job very seriously. They had arranged to meet outside the hospital gates at eight that evening and he was really looking forward to it.

He walked upstairs and into his room and almost tripped over his suitcase which was parked right behind the door.

'Your goods all in there!' said the landlady, suddenly materializing in the doorway.

'What!'

'I'm not silly!' cried the old one. 'You had woman in my house last night. I pack in all your goods!'

'What? No, I didn't! A woman!'

'Come on, don't tell me. I know. I'm not silly!' She advanced towards him.

'Not me!' he protested, backing away.

'I tell Mister Pernacci no! I say no young man! But no! He say you are nice boy. Steady!' Her angular nose wrinkled in disgust. 'This the way you treat us eh?' She yelled.

He could only shrug. She was eighty eight years of age at least.

'And Mister Clark say he hear noises other times. And I don't believe!'

'Ah he's a liar! Where does he live? Does he live up above?' He could not restrain a grin appearing on his face.

'Aah please please, do not be cheeky with me.'

'I'm not being cheeky. But it's not very nice throwing somebody out into the street like this is it!'

The landlady poked his back as she followed him downstairs. 'Don't talk,' she said, 'not very nice with woman in my house. Never before in many many years! Think of your mother! No, I think you never do that!'

'I'm a young man Missus Pernacci you must expect it.' He opened the door but paused. 'Surely you can at least think it over?'

'No. Come on. Out you go. Can't behave like this in people's houses!'

He shook his head.

'You must mend yourself,' she continued. 'Now please go. Mister Pernacci be very angry with you!'

'No he'll not!'

'Yes yes, he will.' Her old eyes widened at him. 'Now cheerio please.'

'Cheerio!' he called but the door slammed shut.

The rain was falling steadily when he came lugging the suitcase round the corner at eight p.m. She was surprised to see it when she came out the gates.

Nice to be nice

Strange thing wis it stertit oan a Wedinsday, A mean nothin ever sterts oan a Wedinsday kis it's the day afore pey day an A'm ey skint. Mibby git a buckshee pint roon the *Anchor* bit that's aboot it. Anywey it wis eftir 9 an A wis thinkin aboot gin hame kis a hidny a light whin Boab McCann threw us a dollar an A boat masel an auld Erchie a pint. The auld yin hid 2 boab ay his ain so A took it an won a couple a gemms a dominoes. Didny win much bit enough tae git us a hauf boattle a Lanny. Tae tell ye the truth A'm no fussy fir the wine bit auld Erchie'll guzzle till it comes oot his ears, A'm tellin ye. A'll drink it mine ye bit if A've goat a few boab A'd rethir git a hauf boattle a whisky thin 2 ir 3 boattles a magic. No auld Erchie. Anywey — nice tae be nice — every man tae his ain, comes 10 and we wint roon the coarner tae git inty the wine. Auld Erchie waantit me tae go up tae his place bit Jesus Christ it's like annickers midden up therr. So anywey A think A git aboot 2 moothfus oot it afore it wis done kis is A say, whin auld Erchie gits stertit oan that plonk ye canny haud him. The auld cunt's a disgrace.

A left him ootside his close an wint hame. It wis gittin cauld an A'm beginnin tae feel it merr these days. That young couple wir hinging aboot in the close in at it as usual. Every night in the week an A'm no kiddin ye! Thir parents waant tae gie thim a room tae thirsel, A mean everybody's young wance — know whit A mean. They waant tae git merrit anywey. Jesus Christ they young yins nooadays iv goat thir heid screwed oan merr thin we ever hid, an the sooner they git merrit the better. Anyhow, as usual they didny even notice me goin up the sterr.

Bit it's Betty Sutherland's lassie an young Peter Craig — A knew his faither an they tell me he's almost as hard as his auld man wis. Still, the perr iv thim ir winchin near enough 6 month noo so mibby she's knoaked some sense inty his heid. Good luck tae thim, A hope she his, a nice wee lassie — aye, an so wis her maw.

A hid tae stoap 2 flerrs up tae git ma breath back. A'm no as bad as A wis bit A'm still no right; that bronchitis — Jesus Christ, A hid it bad. Hid tae stoap work cause iv it. Good joab A hid tae, the lorry drivin. Hid tae chuck it bit. Landid up in the Western Infirmary. Nae breath at aw. Couldny fuckin breathe. Murder it wis. Still, A made it tae the toap okay. A stey in a room an kitchen an inside toilet an it's no bad kis A only pey 6 an a hauf a month fir rent an rates. A hear they're tae come doon right enough bit A hope it's no fir a while yit kis A'll git buggir aw bein a single man. If she wis here A'd git a coarpiration hoose bit she's gone fir good an anywey they coarpiration hooses urny worth a fuck. End up peying a haunful a week an dumped oot in the wilds! Naw, no me. No even a pub ir buggir aw! Naw, they kin stick them.

Wance in the hoose A pit oan the kettle fir a pot iv tea an picked up a book. A'm no much ay a sleeper at times an A sometimes end up readin aw night. Hauf an oor later the door goes. Funny — A mean A dont git that minny visitors.

Anywey it wis jist young Tony who'd firgoat his key, he wis wi that wee mate ay his an a perr a burds. Christ, whit dae ye dae? Invite thim in? Well A did — nice tae be nice — an anywey thir aw right they two; sipposed tae be a perr a terraways bit A ey fun Tony aw right, an his mate's his mate. The young yins ir aw right if ye lea thim alane. A've eywis maintained that. Gie thim a chance fir fuck sake. So A made thim at hame although it meant me hivin tae sit oan a widdin cherr kis A selt the couch a couple a months ago kis ay that auld cunt Erchie an his troubles. They four hid perred aff an were sittin oan the ermcherrs. They hid brung a cerry-oot wi thim so A goat the glesses an it turned oot no a bad wee night, jist chattin away aboot poalitics an the hoarses an aw that. A quite enjoyed it

31

although mine you A wis listenin merr thin A wis talkin, bit that's no unusual. An wan iv the burds didny say much either an A didny blame her kis she knew me. She didny let oan bit. See A used to work beside her man — aye she's nae chicken, bit nice tae be nice, she isny a bad lookin lassie. An A didny let oan either.

Anywey, must a been near 1 a cloak whin Tony gits me oan ma ain an asks me if they kin aw stey the night. Well some might ay thoat they wir takin liberties bit at the time it soundit reasonable. A said they kid sleep ben the room an A'd sleep here in the kitchen. Tae tell the truth A end up spennin the night here in the cherr hell iv a loat these days. Wan minute A'm sittin readin an the nix it's 6 a cloak in the moarnin an ma neck's as stiff as a poker ir somethin. A've bin thinkin ay movin the bed frae the room inty the kitchen recess anywey — might as well — A mean it looks hell iv a daft hivin wan double bed an nothin else. Aye, an A mean nothin else, sep the lino. Flogged every arra fuckin thin thit wis in the room an A sippose if A wis stuck A kid flog the bed. Comes tae that A kid even sell the fuckin room ir at least rent it oot. They Pakies wid jump at it — A hear they're sleepin twinty handit tae a room an mine's is a big room. Still, good luck tae thim, they work hard fir their money, an if they dont good luck tae thim if they kin git away wi it.

A goat a couple a blankets an that bit tae tell the truth A wisny even tired. Sometimes whin A git a taste ay that bevy that's me — awake tae aw oors. An A've goat tae read then kis thir's nae point sterring at the waw — nothin wrang wi the waw right enough, me an Tony done it up last spring, aye, an done no a bad joab tae. Jist the kitchen bit kis A didny see the point ay doin up the room wi it only hivin wan double bed fir furniture. He pit up a photy iv Jimi Hendrix oan the waw, a poster. A right big yin.

Whit's the story wi the darkie oan the waw? says auld Erchie the first time he comes up eftir it wis aw done. Wis the greatest guitarist in the World ya auld cunt ye! says Tony an he grabs the auld yin's bunnet an flings it oot the windy. First time A've seen yir heid, he says. Nae wunnir ye keep it covered.

The Erchie filla wisny too pleased. Mine you A hidny seen him much wioot that bunnet masell. He's goat 2 ir 3 strans a herr stretchin frae the back iv his heid tae the front. An the bunnet wis still lyin therr oan the pavement whin he wint doon fir it. Even the dugs widny go near it. It's a right dirty lookin oabjict bit then so's the auld yin's heid.

Anywey, A drapped aff to sleep eventually — wioot chinegin, well it wid be broo day the morra an A wis waantin tae git up early wi them bein therr an aw that.

Mibby it wis the bevy A dont know bit the nix thin Tony's pullin ma erm, staunin oor me wi a letter frae the tax an A kid see it wisny a form tae fill up. A'd nae idear whit it wis so A opind it right away and oot faws a cheque fir 42 quid. Jesus Christ A near collapsed. A mean A've been oan the broo fir well oor a year, an naebody gits money eftir a year. Therr ye ur bit — 42 quid tae prove me wrang. No bad eh!

Wiv knoaked it aff Stan, shouts Tony, grabbin it oot ma haun.

Well A mean A've seen a good few quid in ma days whit wi the hoarses an aw that bit it the time it wis like winnin the pools so it wis. A'm no kiddin ye. Some claes an mibby a deposit tae try fir that new HGV yiv goat tae git afore ye kin drive the lorries nooadays.

Tony gits his mate an the burds up an tells thim it's time tae be gaun an me an him wint doon the road fir a breakfist. We winty a cafe an hid the works an Tony boat a *Sporting Chronicle* an we dug oot a couple. Well he did kis A've merr ir less chucked it these days. Aye, long ago. Disny bother me much noo bit it wan time A couldny walk by a bettin shoap. Anywey, nae merr ay that. An Tony gammils enough fir the baith ay us. Course he wid bet oan 2 flies climbin a waw whirras A wis eywis a hoarsy man. Wance ir twice A mibby took an intrist in a dug bit really it wis eywis the hoarses wi me. A sippose the gammlin wis the real reason how the wife fukt aff an left me. Definitely canny blame her bit. I mean she near enough stuck it 30 year by Christ. Nae merr ay that.

A hid it aw figird oot how tae spen the cash. Tony wint fir his broo money an I decidet jist tae go hame fir merr iv a think.

Whin A goat therr Big Moira wis in daein the cleanin up fir me bit she wisny long in puttin oan a cup a tea. Jist aboot every time ye see her she's either drinkin tea ir jist aboot tae pit it oan. So wir sittin an she's bletherin away good style aboot her weans an the rest ay it whin aw iv a sudden she tells me she's gittin threw oot her hoose — ay an the 4 weans wi her. Said she goat a letter tellin her. Canny dae it A says.

Aye kin they no, says Moira. The coarpiration kin dae whit they like Stan.

Well A didny need Moira tae tell me that bit A also knew thit they widny throw a single wummin an 4 weans oot inty the street. A didny tell her bit — in case she thoat A wis oan therr side ir somethin. Big Moira's like that. A nice lassie, bit she's ey gittin thins inty her heid aboot people, so A said nothin. She telt me she wint straight up tae see the manager bit he wisny therr so she seen this young filla an he telt her she'd hivty git oot an it wisny cause ay her debts (she owes a few quid arrears). Naw, it seems 2 ir 3 ay her neighbours wir up complainin aboot her weans makin a mess in the close an shoutin an bawlin ir somethin. An thir's nothin ye kin dae aboot it, he says tae her.

Well that wis a diffrint story an A wis beginnin tae believe her. She wis aw fir sortin it oot wi the neighbours bit A telt her no tae bother till she fun oot fir certain whit the score wis. Anywey, eftir gittin the weans aff her maw she wint away hame. So Moira hid tae git oot ay her hoose afore the end ay the month. Course whether they'd cerry oot the threat ir no wis a diffrint story — surely the publicity alane wid pit thim aff. A must admit the merr A wis thinkin aboot it the angrier A wis gettin. Naw — nice tae be nice — ye canny go aboot pittin the fear a death inty folk, speshly a wummin like Moira. She's a big stroang lassie bit she's nae man tae back her up. An whin it comes tae talkin they bastirts up it Clive House wid run rings roon ye. Naw, A know whit like it is. Treat ye like A dont know whit so they dae. A wis gittin too worked up so I jist opind a book an tried tae firget aboot it. Anywey, A fell asleep in the cherr — oot like a light an didny wake up till well eftir 5 a cloak.

Ma neck wis hell iv a stiff bit A jist shoved oan the jaiket an wint doon the road.

The *Anchor* wis busy an A saw auld Erchie staunin near the dominoe table wherr he usually hings aboot if he's skint in case emdy waants a drink. Kis he sometimes gits a drink himsel fir gaun. A wint straight tae the bar an asked John fir 2 gless a whisky an a couple a hauf pints an whin A went tae pey the man A hid fuck aw bar some smash an a note sayin, Give you it back tomorrow, Tony.

40 quid! A'll gie ye it the morra! Jesus Christ Almighty. An he wis probly hauf wey oor tae Ashfield right noo. An therrs me staunin therr like a fuckin numbskull! 40 notes! Well well well, an it wisny the first time. A mean he disny let me doon, he's eywis goat it merr ir less whin he says he will bit nice tae be nice, know whit A mean! See A gave him a sperr key whin we wir daein up the kitchen an A let him hing oan tae it eftirwirds kis sometimes he's naewherr tae kip. Moira's maw's git the other yin in case ay emergencies an aw that. Bit Tony drapped me right in it. John's staunin therr behind the bar sayin nothin while A'm readin the note a hauf dozen times. The bill comes tae aboot 70 pence — aboot 6 boab in chinge. A leans oor the counter an whispers sorry an tells him A've come oot wioot ma money.

Right Stan it's aw right, he says, A'll see ye the morra — dont worry aboot it.

Whit a showin up. A gave the auld yin his drink oor an wint oor tae sit oan ma tod. Tae be honest, A wisny in the mood fir either Erchie's patter or the dominoes. 40 sovvies! Naw, the merr A thoat aboot it the merr A knew it wis oot ay order. Okay, he didny know A firgoat aboot ma broo money kis ay me hivin that kip — bit it's nae excuse, nae excuse. Aw he hid tae dae wis wake me up an A'd iv ay gave him the rest if wis needin it that bad. The trouble wis A knew the daft bastirt'd dae somethin stupit tae git it back if he wound up losin it aw at the dugs. Jesus Christ, aw the worries iv the day whit wi big Moira an the weans an noo him. An whit wid happen if they did git chucked oot! Naw, A couldny see it. Ye never know bit. I

35

decidet tae take a walk up tae the coarpiration masell. A kin talk whin A waant tae, bit right enough whin they bastirts up therr git stertit they end up blindin ye wi science. Anywey, I git inty John fir a hanfill oan the strength ay ma broo money an wint hame early wi a haufboattle an a big screwtap wioot sayin a word tae auld Erchie.

Tony still hidny showed up by the Monday, that wis 4 days so A knew A'd nae chance ay seein him till he hid the cash in his haun ready fir me. An it wis obvious he might hiv tae go tae the thievin gemms inty the bargin an thir wis nothin A could dae aboot it, A'd be too late. Big Moira's maw came up the sterr tae see me the nix moarnin. Word hid come aboot her hivin tae be oot the hoose by the 30th ir else they'd take immediate action. The lassie's maw wis in a hell iv a state kis she couldny take thim in wi her only hivin a single end. A offirt tae help oot bit it didny make matters much better. An so I went roon as minny factors as A could. Nae luck bit. Nothin, nothin at aw. Ach A didny expect much anyhow tae be honest aboot it. Hopeless. I jist telt her maw A'd take a walk up Clive House an see if they'd mibby offer some alternit accommodation — an no tae worry kis they'd never throw thim inty the street. Single wummin wi 4 weans! Naw, the coarpiration widny chance that yin. Imagine expectin her to pey that kinna rent tae! Beyond a joke so it is. An she says the rooms ir damp an aw that, and whin she cawed in the sanitry they telt her tae open the windaes an let the err in. The middle ay the fuckin winter! Let the err in! Ay, an as soon's her back's turnt aw the villains ir in screwin the meters an whit no. A wis ragin. An whin A left the hoose oan the Wedinsday moarnin A wis still hell iv a angry. Moira wis waantin tae come up wi me bit A telt her naw it might be better if A wint oan ma tod.

So up A goes an A queued up tae see the manager bit he wisny available so A saw the same wan Moira saw, a young filla cawed Mr Frederick. A telt him whit wis whit bit he wisny bothrin much an afore A'd finished he jumps in sayin that in the furst place he'd explained everythin tae Mrs Donnelly (Moira) an the department hid sent her oot letters which she'd no taken the trouble tae answer — an in the second place it wis nane iv ma business. Then he shouts: Nix please.

A loast ma rag at that an the nix thin A know A'm lyin here an that wis yesterday, Thursday — A'd been oot the gemm since A grabbed the wee cunt by the throat. Lucky A didny strangle him tae afore A collapsed.

Dont even know if A'm gittin charged an tae be honest A couldny gie 2 monkeys whether A am ir no. Bit that's nothin. Moira's maw comes up tae visit me this moarnin an gies me the news. Young Tony gits back Wedinsday dinner time bit no findin me goes doon tae Moira's maw an gits telt the story. He says nothin tae her bit jist goes right up tae the coarpiration wherr he hings aboot till he finds oot whit's whit wi the clerks, then whin Mr Frederick goes hame a gang iv young thugs ir supposed ta iv set aboot him an done him up pretty bad bit the polis only manages tae catch wan ay thim an it turns oot tae be Tony who disny even run aboot wi embdy sem sometimes that wee mate iv his. So therr it is an A'll no really know the score till the nix time A see him. An big Moira an the weans, as far as A hear they've still naewherr tae go either, A mean nice tae be nice, know whit A mean.

The bevel

When I woke up the sun was already quite strong and it was clammy in the caravan; also it seemed like the midges had started biting. I had to rise. Chas was snoring in his bunk but in the other there was neither sound nor movement amongst the big heap of blankets. I gave up worrying about that a few days earlier. I struck a match and lit a cigarette. Time to get up: I shouted.

Chas moved; he blinked then muttered unintelligibly. I told him it was going to be another scorcher. He nodded. He peered at the big heap of blankets and raised a foot and let it crash down. An arm reached out from the blankets, it groped about the floor for the spectacles beneath the bunk. I picked them up. Then Sammy appeared with his other hand shielding his eyes. I passed him the spectacles and also a cigarette. When we inhaled he went into a coughing paroxysm. Jesus Christ, he managed to gasp.

Never mind, just think of the bacon and eggs, and these boiled tomatoes.

Chas had pulled his jeans out from underneath his bunk and was dressing. He glanced at Sammy: Some smells coming from your side last night.

Ah give us peace.

Chas is right, I said, fucking ridiculous. I'm complaining to Joe about it.

Ah shut up. Anyhow, when you get to my age it's all you're bloody good for.

Chas grinned. A different story last night — you and that

auld wife of yours! I could hardly get to sleep for thinking about it. Aye and I'll be telling her what you said next time I see her.

Last time I let yous get me drunk, chuckled Sammy. I'll no have a secret left by the time we get back down the road . . . And he tugged the blankets up over his shoulders. Me and Chas went into the kitchenette for a wash. When we returned Sammy was sitting up and knotting the laces on his boots, ready to leave. Ach, he said, I cant be bothered washing. I'll wait till we get to the canteen.

Clatty auld bastard, I said.

Not at all. It's to do with the natural oils son — that's how yous pair keep getting hit by the midges.

Rubbish, said Chas, you're a clatty auld cunt.

We parked in the place behind the canteen. Nobody was around. It was a Saturday, but even so, the three of us were always first into the canteen each morning. The woman smiled. As she dished out the grub she said, You lot were the worse for wear last night.

Aye, said Chas, what happened to that dance you promised us?

Dance! you couldnt walk never mind dance. You keelies, you're all the same.

Aw here wait a minute, cried Sammy. Less of that race-relations patter if you dont mind.

It's these teuchters Sammy, I said, they're all the same so they are. Sooner we see a subway the better.

Away with your subways! The woman was piling the boiled tomatoes and bacon onto my plate . . . What're you wanting subways for?

Never mind what we're wanting subways for! Chas chuckled.

Aye hen, grinned Sammy, you can do a lot on a subway!

Is that so! well just dont be trying any of that tonight.

We carried our trays across to the table near the big windows. Sammy returned them to the rack once we had taken off our stuff. Actually, he said, I dont think I'll go to the club the night.

Thank Christ for that!

Naw son seriously.

But dont count on it, grinned Chas. He winked as he sliced a piece of bacon and dipped it into the egg yolk. He'll be there spoiling everything as per fucking usual.

Naw Chas honest. I'll have to take a look at the car. That bloody chinking sound's beginning to annoy me — besides which, we're spending too much on the bevy so we are. O Christ, he added, this food, it's bloody marvellous. I've never eaten like this in my puff.

While he spoke me and Chas were automatically covering our plates. Sammy seldom put in his teeth this early.

I've got to agree with you, said Chas, it's some grub right enough.

I snorted. I'll never know what yous pair got married for.

Sammy grinned. Will you listen to the boy!

After the second mug of tea we went back to the car to get the working-gear. Even when Sammy opened the boot the smell of it hit us; first thing in the morning was always bad. The boilersuits we had had to borrow from the factory stores, they were stiff and reeking of sweat; probably they had been left behind years ago by some squad of subcontractors.

Chas had slapped himself on the wrist suddenly and he turned up the palm of his hand to show us the remains of a midge. Look, he said, a bit of fucking dust. Aye Sammy, we definitely need a tin of cream or something.

I'll see Joe.

O good, I said.

Sammy glanced at me.

The chlorine tank we were working on stood at the very rear of the factory, not too far from the lochside. Its lining was being renewed. We had to strip away the old stuff to prepare the way. The tank was about 40 feet high and about 18 in diameter. On top was a small outlet through which the scaffolders had passed down their equipment; a narrow walkway separated it from a factory outbuilding. There was also a very small tunnel at the foot which us three had to use; it was quite a tight fit, especially for Sammy.

To allow us maximum daylight the scaffolders had erected the interior staging with minimum equipment. The platforms on which we worked were spaced about 8 feet apart. When we finished stripping a section of old lining we had to shift most of the planks and boards to the next, to make it safe to work on. But generated light was also necessary. In fact it would probably have suited us to have had the maximum scaffolding stuff rather than extra daylight. It was safe enough but we had to be careful; since the tank was circular the platforms couldnt cover the entire 18 feet. Chas had spotted a potential problem in connection with this. It was a bevel in one side. He had pointed it out to us yesterday evening.

While he went off to swtich on the compressor I fiddled around with the air-hoses, giving Sammy a chance to sneak on ahead into the tunnel; somewhere inside was a place where he planked the chisels and other stuff. He was a bit neurotic about thieving and wouldnt even tell us where he kept it all.

It was a fair climb to the section we were on. One of the snags of the job was this continual climbing. The chisels kept on bouncing out the hammer nozzles and it seemed like it was my job to go and get them — and when they fell they always fell to the bottom of the tank. Once Chas arrived we adjusted the hammers onto the air-hoses and fixed on the chisels then one by one we triggered off. Half an hour later we stopped. Earlier in the week I got a spark in my right eye; while along at the First-aid I discovered we were not supposed to stay longer than 30 minutes without at least having a quarter of an hour break out in the open.

Sammy had gone off to make his morning report by telephone to the depot. Back at the lochside he explained how Joe had been unable to make it up yesterday. They had needed him for an urgent job. But he would definitely arrive some time today.

Is that all? I said, What I means is did they no even apologise?

Aye, what would've happened if we were skint! said Chas.

Well we werent skint.

That's no the point but.

I know it's no the bloody point. Sammy sniffed, then he nudged the spectacles up on his nose a bit. The trouble with you son you're a Commie.

Naw I'm no — a good Protestant.

Sammy snorted. After a moment he said, I could always have seen that whatsisname, Williams, he would've subbed us a few quid.

Aye and that'd be us begging again!

He's right, said Chas. They must be sick of the sight of us in this fucking place. Fucking boilersuits and breathing-masks by Christ we're never done.

Aw stop your moaning.

Heh, you definitely no going to the club the night?

None of your business.

Chas grinned, Course he's going. Saturday night! Dirty auld bastard, he couldnt survive without sniffing a woman.

Ah well, said Sammy, nothing wrong with sniffing. And I'll tell you something . . .

We know we know — when you get to your age it's all your fucking good for.

Sammy laughed.

Joe turned up in the afternoon, during one of the breaks out the tank. We were at the shore, skliffing pebbles on the surface of the water. The last time he came we were doing exactly the same thing. The time before that we had been standing gabbing to one of the storemen, and it was pointless trying to explain about conning the fellow out of a couple of new boilersuits. Joe never heard explanations. His eyes would glaze over.

Heh Joe, I said, the First-aid people said we were supposed to get a quarter of an hour break every half hour, because of the fumes, the chlorine and that.

Is that right . . . Joe nodded. He was lighting a cigarette, then chipping the match into the loch.

That's what they said.

Aye, it's kind of muggy . . . He gazed towards the head of the loch where several small boats were sailing north, the gannets flying behind and making their calls. He sniffed and glanced at his wristwatch, and glanced at Sammy. Fancy showing me your bevel? he said.

Aye Joe.

They walked up the slope. We waited a bit before following. Joe had gone off alone, and Sammy paused for us to catch up with him. He's away to see if whatsisname's arrived yet — he's supposed to be coming in to see the bevel . . . Pulling a rag from a pocket he wiped his brow and neck, and then wrapped it round his head like a sweatband. Must be hitting the 80's, he grunted. I'll tell you something, we're better off in the fucking tank.

What did he say about it? said Chas. Did he say anything?

Sammy looked at him.

The bevel I mean.

Aw aye. Naw, he'll have to have a look.

Heh, I said, Sammy! d'you notice the way he went *your* bevel; *your* bevel. As if you'd put the fucking thing there yourself.

Ach it's just his way . . . Sammy continued walking.

Another thing, I said, I bet you he asks that cunt Williams about the quarter of an hour breaks.

No danger, said Chas.

In fact it wouldnt surprise me if he knew about it in the first place — just forgot to fucking tell us.

As usual, muttered Chas.

For God sake! Sammy stopped and glared at us.

Well no wonder Sammy, sometimes he treats us as if we were the three fucking stooges.

The boy's right, said Chas. I notice he's no saying anything about the wages.

They'll be in his bloody car.

Aye and they'll stay there as long as possible, just in case we nick away for a pint or something.

Sammy's face reddened; he nudged the spectacles up on his

nose. He turned and strode on to the tunnel. We watched him crawling inside.

Chas shrugged. We've upset him now.

Ach, no wonder. He's letting Joe take the piss out him.

He's no really.

Well how come he's still climbing scaffolding at his fucking age? he should be permanent down in the depot.

True. Chas sniffed, Come on — we better go and show the auld cunt we still love him.

He was pounding away with the hammer. He ignored us while we were preparing our stuff. Finally he switched off the power. About bloody time and all, he said, get cracking. I thought yous had went for a pint right enough!

How could we! it's your fucking round.

Sammy shook his head and turned back to the wall of the tank again, and triggered off. Chas winked at me. We worked on steadily. Then without having to ask I knew we were past the half hour. I saw Chas pause to demist the goggles he wore; he adjusted his breathing-mask and shrugged when I gestured at my wrist. We continued with the hammers.

About 5 minutes later the signal came from below; somebody was climbing the scaffolding. Both Joe and Williams. We stopped work. Sammy went off to show them the bevel and me and Chas had a smoke, sitting on the platform. We could hear snatches of their conversation. Williams said something about Monday being a Bank Holiday and Chas started laughing quietly. I fucking knew it, he whispered, we've knocked it right off.

What d'you mean?

He shook his head, then he whispered: You still fancy having a go at the Ben?

Fucking right I do, climbing it, aye. How?

Ssh.

Heh, heh yous two! Joe was calling. We got up and climbed to the next platform. He and Williams stood beside each other. A couple of yards away Sammy stared at the floor, puffing at a cigarette and scratching his head. Joe gestured us closer and

said, I think we've got it beat. Look . . . he pointed at a couple of
planks. Now Chas, if you and Sammy stand at the bottom end
of them the boy'll be able to go out and do the lining.

What?

See look . . . Joe tugged Chas by the elbow who then stepped
aside while Joe placed the planks one on the other; he pushed
them like that out over the gap being caused by the bevelled side
of the tank. See what I mean? he said. And he wiped his hands.

Eh . . .

Look Chas . . .

But before Joe could continue Williams had stepped
forward. The thing is, he said, the weight. You and Sammy,
together you must make about 3 or 4 of the boy. If you two
stand on the bottom end of the planks he'll be able to get out at
the top. You'll balance him no bother.

Chas didnt reply and I glanced at Sammy.

Save us a hell of a lot of bother too, added Joe. What d'you
think?

Eh . . .

Joe sniffed and turned: What about yourself Sammy?

Ah, I'm no too sure Joe, being honest.

I think it'll work fine, said Williams. He's light — you two'll
balance him easy.

We could use three planks if you like, said Joe.

O naw. Sammy glanced at him: You couldnt use three
planks. Naw Joe they'd just spread, it'd have to be two.

Aye . . . Joe nodded. He took out a packet of cigarettes and
offered them round everybody. What d'you reckon? he said to
Chas.

Eh . . . Chas sniffed. Then he shook his head slowly. I'm no
sure Joe.

Worth a try but eh? Joe turned to me. Eh young yin? what
d'you think? could you give it a go?

After a moment Williams said, Wait a minute, I've got a
suggestion. What weight d'you think I am?

I shrugged.

Well I'm a good bit heavier than you though, agreed? Now

45

look, if you and one of your mates take one end then I'll go out the other. Well say the three of you.

That's better, grinned Joe.

Williams tapped himself on the belly and chuckled, Dont remind me! No, seriously . . . He looked to Sammy and Chas. The three of you to balance me as opposed to you two balancing the boy, what d'you say?

At least to give it a try, said Joe.

It's no the same thing, I said.

Yes, said Williams, it's only a try though.

Aye but the hammer. Sammy said, It's the hammer Mr Williams — once it starts vibrating and the rest of it.

I know, fair enough.

It's different from just standing there, I said.

Joe cleared his throat.

Tell you what, said Williams, while I'm out I'll give it a blast with a hammer, will that do you?

I didnt reply.

Ah come on, said Joe.

But it's no the same thing.

We're no saying it's the same thing.

I just want to see how it works, shrugged Williams.

There was a moment's silence then Sammy came across the platform. No harm in seeing how it works, he said. Come on Chas . . . He also waved me forward onto the planks. I hesitated but he nodded me on. He stood at the back, me in the middle, Chas to the front.

Right then Tom, said Joe to Williams, and he passed him a hammer with the chisel already fixed onto the nozzle. You ever worked one before?

Dont tell me — you pull the trigger! He took the hammer, checked it was securely attached to the air-hose then gave it a short burst. He manoeuvred his way along the planks, moving out on the top end, right over the gap at the bevel. Okay? he said.

Fine, called Sammy.

He put the chisel to the lining and triggered it off; the planks spread and we lost our footing, the hammer clattering and Williams yelled, but he managed to twist and get half onto the edge of the platform, clinging there with his mouth gaping open. Joe and Chas were already to him and clutching his arms, then me and Sammy were there and helping. When he got up onto the platform he sat for a long time, until his breathing approached something more normal. Nobody spoke during it all. His face was really grey. Joe had taken his cigarettes out and passed them round again. When he had given Williams a light he said, How you feeling Tom?

Williams nodded.

We continued smoking without speaking.

Eventually he glanced at Joe: Think I could do with a breath of fresh air.

Joe nodded. The four of us climbed down with him coming in between; he was still shaky but he managed it okay. When we came out of the tunnel he said, Jesus Christ . . . He smiled and shook his head at us. Joe went with him.

Down at the lochside Joe reappeared, and distributed the wages and subsistence money. While we checked the contents against the pay-slips he gazed towards the foot of the loch. The mountain peaks were distinct. Below the summit of the Ben a helicopter was hovering. Joe watched it for a time. Good place this, he said, a rare view.

Full of tourists but. Sammy shook his head. Can hardly get moving for Germans.

Joe nodded, he lit a cigarette. Pity about that fucking bevel, he said, we'll no manage to get the scaffolders out till Tuesday at the earliest — probably Wednesday . . . He glanced in the direction of Sammy.

Aye.

Puts us back.

Sammy nodded. Then he sniffed. Mind you Joe there's a fair bit of clearing up we can be getting on with — all that stuff we've stripped and that.

Aye . . . Joe inhaled on the cigarette. It's a nuisance but.

How's thingwi — that whatsisname, Williams?

Aw he's fine, fine. A bit shaky.

Sammy nodded, he nudged the spectacles on his nose.

Heh look at that! Joe had turned and he pointed out to where a motor launch and a water skier could be seen. Christ sake! he said. And he stood watching them for a long while. At last he glanced at his wristwatch. He turned and snorted.

Sammy looked at him.

So where is it the night? the social club?

Doubt it Joe — bloody car, it's acting up again.

Joe nodded.

What about yourself?

Aw! The time I get back down the road . . . He sniffed and glanced back at the loch, then he said, I suppose, I suppose . . . He glanced at his wristwatch. Okay Sammy, mind and phone in as soon as the scaffolders arrive.

Will do.

And eh — just do as much as you can, in the tank and that.

Aye well I mean that clearing Joe . . .

Once he had gone the three of us continued sitting there, smoking, not talking for a while.

Charlie

Charlie had one suit and he wore it all times. He worked for a stone-cleaning outfit travelling throughout England and Wales, and in his situation this was perfect. He owed a fortune in maintenance back payments for a wife and three weans he had left up in Lanarkshire somewhere. He was self-employed. In theory he subcontracted himself out to the stone-cleaning outfit -- something like that. What it did mean was that he was more or less untraceable. I was living in digs in Manchester at the time, had just survived a lean spell and now moved into the house paying a week's cash in advance. Not a bad place. Long-distance lorrydrivers inhabited it mostly. During the weekends few people were around, and until Charlie arrived I had the lounge and dining room virtually to myself. Charlie seldom went anywhere except to his work, Friday being the only day throughout the week he would not stay for overtime beyond 7 p.m. And before entering the house that evening he always spent an extra couple of minutes slapping the grey dust from out of his suit. After eating his meal he stepped down to the local pub but rarely drank more than five pints of bitter, he had always returned long before closing time. I doubt if he particularly enjoyed drinking beer. I think he just needed company occasionally, and also to get rid of a couple of quid in a *bona fide* sort of manner — before making it into the betting shop on the Saturday afternoon.

Having received the giro on the Friday morning I was normally skint on the Friday evening and Charlie began taking me along to the boozer where he would buy me the same drink as himself. He always seemed glad to make the move back to the house. The following afternoon I tagged along with him to the betting shop and watched the performance. It was dismal.

Once or twice I had gained a few bob on the Friday afternoon and so could have a go on my own but this was rare; the usual thing was my being skint and watching Charlie. He never won. Whatsoever. Never received one solitary return during the weeks I knew him. He bet in permutations to the precise extent of what lay in his pocket. If he had twenty two quid his bet was a £2 *yankee* which at eleven bets would amount to the full £22.00. Twenty six quid and he would place a £2 *canadian* to equal the £26.00. If he had twenty nine quid in his pocket then he would make out the line as a 50 pence *heinz* amounting to £28.50 and toss in the extra 50 pence on the accumulator bet. It had to be that his pocket contained nothing bar pennies after the day's business. Anybody happening to observe his bets would say something like: When Charlie knocks it off, he'll do it in a Big Way.

In the betting shop the woman behind the counter used to give him a nice smile. Nothing to do with his being a loser because she had no percentage in the take, she was only a counter-hand. The landlady also liked him. He was always punctual for meals, said a good morning, washed before getting to the dining room table. And she delivered him up the largest portions, the choicest cuts, the additional rashers of bacon and the rest of it. If he was aware of this treatment he never acknowledged it that I knew about. All the lorrydrivers had noticed though. They could be seen weighing up the number of spuds they had in comparison to Charlie, but nothing was ever said — even in a joke.

His failure to get a return on his betting shop outlay was no failure in this sense: he planned it. He bought weekly travel passes and hoarded the dowp-ends of each cigarette he smoked though he didnt give this as a reason for smoking plain cigarettes. I used to mix these dowps in with my own tobacco and roll him a decent smoke because he never managed to learn how to handroll himself a cigarette, and never even bothered to buy one of these cheap rolling devices you can get. He said: I've thought about it. Just cant seem to come round to it somehow.

The way he lost his money depressed me. And yet only in retrospect; there was something about those bets he made — they always seemed to show promise. The majority of his selected runners would be going in televised races but he made a point of leaving the last horse to be in an event scheduled to run later in the afternoon. This was for the sake of his nerves. Imagine having four winners, he said, and having to *watch* that fifth yin run its race out on the telly. Naw. I couldnt stand that.

There was no danger of this ever happening. The nearest he ever got was one afternoon when his first runner romped home at 16/1. And before the runners came *under orders* for the next he was up and downstairs from his room to the lavatory about ten times. When it was eventually revealed to him that his bet had lost as usual he said: Bastard. Fucked again.

And we settled down to watch television or read books till the following Friday, tapping smokes from the lorrydrivers and the wee woman who helped out in the kitchen, once my tobacco and his dowp-ends had finally run out.

Considering the amount he was punting I told him it might be best to stick it all down on a single horse — possibly spending the whole of Saturday morning just studying form to pick out one stonewall certainty. That's a thought, he said. And the following Saturday I spent the whole morning huddled over *The Sporting Life* to come up with three possibles, any one of which I fancied strongly. He agreed about their chances when he came back from work about midday. Eventually he did choose one. But only to include it in a permutation. The horse ran in the first race, and it finished second, beaten only by the favourite. The thing had definitely been unlucky not to win in my opinion. But Charlie said: See what I mean? That would've been me fucked before I'd usually have been starting!

And no matter that his next four selections all finished well down the field, he reckoned the point had been settled. I never made a similar suggestion. It did depress me though. He knew nothing at all about horse racing and yet week in week out there he was punting to the limit of his pocket. And considering the maintenance money he owed he was also punting to the limit of his wife and three weans' pockets. He never spoke of this. After the fourth pint one Friday evening I asked him about them. Closed book that, he said, shaking his head.

About five weeks after his arrival he invited me for a game of snooker instead of crossing the road to the boozer. We went to a place in Oxford Road. And without ever having seen me play, just as he prepared to break the reds, he said: Make it for a pound eh!

I told him no. As usual I was skint, and apart from anything else was already relying on him for the cost of the table. Doesnt matter, he said. You can pay me next week.

Charlie broke the balls and I won easily, that game and the rest. He was a very bad player. Five games we played in two hours which meant I had won myself five quid. I told him it was hopeless. I'm too good for you Charlie, I said.

He shook his head: Not really. I'm just an unlucky bastard. I'll win it back off you next Friday.

Next Friday I took him for another fiver; and each successive Friday till he left for Folkestone was the same. He played a mad game. Mighty swipes. No positional play. No potting ability. No nothing. Whenever he sunk a red this red would have cannoned off maybe half a dozen other balls and all of the cushions. It was pathetic. And my own game soon degenerated to his level, although never quite enough to lose. But for the first time in my life I was beginning to consider throwing a game on purpose. I didnt though. It would've been too embarrassing. On each break of each new game Charlie was setting out with this real possibility of winning. It was apparent in his approach to the table. When he messed a shot badly — miscued or actually jumped the cueball off the table altogether through the unchannelled force of his shot — I was beginning to find it difficult to keep from laughing. While bending to retrieve the ball from beneath our table, or somebody else's table, I was having to remain below for a minute to set my face straight. It was becoming too much. Charlie just shrugged. His explanation was: Some fucking luck I'm carrying the night!

But I think he knew I was concealing the laughter, and I was a bit ashamed of it although there was nothing I could do. Eventually I offered three blacks of a start. Never taken a handicap in my life, he said. When I do that I'll know it's time to chuck it.

Two Saturdays before his departure I landed quite a good turn in the betting shop. I passed him a tenner without saying anything. He promptly lost it on a further permutation. And next Friday he returned me the money. What's this? I said. That tenner wasnt a ſoan. I just gave you it.

But he stuck it into the top pocket of my jacket without a word. Come on for a game, he added. I'm due to beat you for a few quid.

Two hours later, with the weekly fiver tucked away in my hip pocket, I told him I was guesting him into town for the rest of the night. Maybe go up a casino or something. Not me, he said.

Fuck sake Charlie you've been buying me drink and keeping me going since you got here.

Doesnt mean I've got to go into the town, he said.

The following day I gave him a tenner after the last race but still he wouldnt go into town so I went in by myself.

During the coming week I was working out methods of not taking his money. I had finished my tea and was sitting back reading the evening paper when he arrived back from work, a bit earlier than usual. Off to Folkestone the night, he said. The job's finished here.

Upstairs he went for a wash and shave. He returned carrying his small suitcase; after eating his meal he bade the cheerios to everybody and stuck his head round the lounge door, he tossed me a ten pound note. I enjoyed playing that snooker, he said. Years since I had a go at it but. A wee bit costly.

The house of an old woman

The hedge was tall but so scrawny we could easily see through it. A huge place. Standing in a jungle of weeds and strange looking sunflowers, big ones which bent at the top and hung backwards to the long grass. It seemed deserted. I hesitated a moment before pushing open the rusty gate. It grated on the cement slab underneath. Freddie and Bob followed me along the narrow path and we stopped at the foot of the flight of steps. I went up and banged the door. And again. Eventually the door opened still on the chain. An old woman gaped out at me. I explained.

Ten pounds a week pay your own lectric! she roared.

I looked at her. She glared at me: Right then, eight and not a penny less! Well? Do you want it or not!

Freddie spoke up from below, asking if we could see it first. But she glared at me again as if I had said it. I shrugged. She pointed at my suitcase and squinted: What did you bring that for if you didnt want to take it? She pursed her lips and added: Right then, but just for a minute because my daughter's coming to get me! She told me they were wanting to take the place — nothing about wanting to see it! Who did the telephone?

Me.

Huh! The door shut and shuffling could be heard, and what sounded like a whole assortment of chains being unhooked. Then the door opened fully and she beckoned me in. She about turned and, with her skirts held in either hand, she walked with a stoop halfway along the enormous and empty lobby. Opening another door she indicated we were to follow her. It was the lounge. The wallpaper reminded me of the fence surrounding the patchwork hedge outside. Above the big mantelpiece a picture had been recently taken down leaving a space which displayed the original design and colours of the wallpaper. An immaculate television set squatted on an orange carpet but apart from that the room was empty. Pointing to both the carpet and television she said: Somebody might come to collect these but you can use them meantime. The bathroom's on the first floor and the big one and the smaller one and above that there's three other rooms all sizes you can make bedrooms out of and in the attic it's a great big room and down here you've got the kitchen next door and the other room and you *cant go into it*. There's the W.C. next to that then the back door leading out to the garden and you should start doing it up. There's fruit out there! She breathed deeply for a bit then cried: Ten pounds plus lectric. And you'll have to pay in advance you know because my daughter'll see that you do.

Turning abruptly she walked to the door but bounced round-about as though expecting to catch us sticking our tongues out. Freddie muttered something to do with it being good value for the money.

Course it's good value! And just you remember about that garden! She said it all directly to me. Once we had wandered about the place we came back downstairs to find her waiting impatiently in the lobby. She wore a fox round the neck of her black coat and a charcoal hat with a large brooch stuck in its crown. Her trousers were amazing though they were probably pantaloons; they had elastic cords fastened at each cuff which were looped round her sturdy walking shoes, to prevent them riding up her legs maybe. These pantaloons were light brown in colours.

Has your daughter not arrived yet? I said. But although I had spoken politely she ignored me. We stood there waiting for her to say something. She acted as if we were not there. It was an uncomfortable feeling. Freddie was first to move. He entered the lounge, and Bob followed. I felt obliged to make some sort of gesture. Eventually I said, Fine — that's fine.

I moved to the door of the lounge and through, and then the door closed firmly behind me. For some reason I let my arm swing backwards as if I had closed it myself.

We sat on the carpet and discussed the situation, but quietly, aware of her standing sentry out in the lobby. Later on the outside door opened, then the lounge door. The daughter appeared, a tall woman who dressed plainly and reminded me of a matron. They left after we paid the advance rent money. Freddie cracked a joke and we laughed. I shuffled the cards and dealt three hands of poker to see who was to get first choice of rooms. I won. I decided on the big one up on the first floor and the other two settled on adjoining ones on the second. It had been a good day. Never for one moment had I really expected to get the place at a rent we could afford. Great value. As I unrolled my sleeping bag I noticed the linoleum was cracked in places and not too clean either. It occurred to me that we should buy carpets before anything else.

Next evening we met in a pub after finishing work. They mentioned they had spent last night in the downstairs lounge. I laughed, but later on, when we were playing cards and drinking cans of beer back in the house, I felt a bit peeved. It was noticed. I passed it off by making some crack about folk being afraid of the dark etc. They laughed with me but insisted it was great having a carpet beneath the sleeping bags. It kept out the cold. They asked if I fancied coming here as well to sleep but I said no. I couldnt be bothered with that. It somehow defeated the purpose of it all, getting a big house and so on. They wanted to carry on with the discussion but I didnt. After a bit we cut for the first bath. I lost. Bob won and when he had gone Freddie said he couldnt be bothered waiting for one and undressed and just got into the sleeping bag. He began exaggerating how cosy it was and soft compared to a dirty cold hard floor, and also how you could chat with company if you couldnt get to sleep.

Rubbish.

I played patience till Bob came back by which time I think Freddie was sleeping. Upstairs in the bathroom I smoked a cigarette while waiting for the tub to fill. Once the taps were turned off I was very aware of how silent everything was. I wished I had been first to think about sleeping downstairs on the lounge carpet. It was a good plan, at least till we started buying stuff to furnish the place. Yet I couldnt really join them now. It had gone a bit far. And it was daft saying that about being scared of the dark. I had meant it as a joke of course and they had taken it the right way. But why had they not come in and got me last night? They said I had been sleeping when they came downstairs but never even looked inside to check, just said they had listened at the door and said my breathing was so regular I couldnt be awake. And the light was off! As if I could somehow wait till I was asleep before switching it out!

I must admit I didnt fancy the idea of sleeping alone the sole occupant of two floors and an attic in a run-down house owned by an old eccentric. But she was not crazy. She had acted the way she had. But old women are notorious. Old people in general — they do odd things.

The bathwater had cooled. No hot left in the tank. Bob must have used more than his fair share. In fact the bathwater was actually getting quite cold. There was a draught coming in under the door which was causing the sleeves of my jumper to sway where it hung on the back of the tall stool. Then the creak! It was terrible hearing it. My body tensed completely. The big cupboard in the corner it came from, and its door moved ajar slightly, and in the shadows I could make out what appeared to be a big coat. It was. I half raised myself up from the bath but I couldnt see it fully. And there couldnt be anyone inside. Otherwise they would have come out. Getting up from the bath I stepped over the side, gathering my clothes without looking in its direction, making my way to the door out. Before opening it I had to relax myself. I stared at my right hand, getting it to stop trembling. I raised it to grip the door handle but did not touch it. My breaths rasped through my teeth. Then I managed to close my fist on the handle but my shoulders had stiffened and I tried to halt my breathing an instant. I could hear nothing but my breaths. I tugged on the handle then the catch released with a sharp click and throwing the door open I dashed forward, cracking my knee against the jamb. I dropped a shoe but didnt stop. I bolted across the corridor and into my room crashing the door shut behind me.

I had suggested clubbing together to buy the largest second-hand carpets we could find, the cost to be borne individually or divided equally, or whatever else they suggested. But no. Objections raised by both. They preferred earlier ideas about buying furniture for each room as each person thought fit. And anyway, they said, they would need at least another fortnight before starting to think about buying anything. To help save I suggested eating in and watching more television but they hummed and they hawed and I could tell they werent too interested. At this point I resolved to bring down the sleeping bag but I could not openly declare it. I hinted the room was freezing cold, it was too big, draughts came in beneath the door and through the patched-up window joints. Neither bothered to comment. One evening I happened to ask whether they still felt the place was good value. Bob grunted something or other and Freddie gave an 'of course' — but in such a way I was made to feel as if I had asked something stupid. Upstairs I went without saying anything further. That same quiet pervading the place. Bob was going for a bath. Now and then the loud crash of the tap being turned on startled me and again startled me when turned off. And these gurgling noises as the water filled the cold-tank.

The sleeping bag was fine, snug enough. Yet if something were to happen my legs would obviously have been restricted. I turned onto my side a lot, a position I could maintain for short periods only because my shoulders ached on the floor, while when lying on my front I would soon become aware of my knees jarring on it. Carpets were definitely essential. A bed would have been even better. And yet I appeared to be the only one interested in buying anything. The draught beneath the door turned an empty cigarette packet halfway about. I was weary. It was not easy to sleep, every bit of me felt exhausted, and the thoughts flying about my brain. And yet things had definitely changed since we had come, there was a coolness being directed against me — in the pub, the bus going to work.

The bathroom door opened and closed then silence for a second before the pitpat downstairs, and later the sound of the lounge door opening and shutting quite firmly. I was honestly glad to be up in my own room, glad not to have succumbed for the sake of a carpet and some sort of safety in numbers. A coat in the cupboard! Felt covering the water tank. What a joke! Laughs all round.

In the cafe one Saturday morning for breakfast I again suggested getting the carpets, maybe starting off buying one at a time and if they liked I would pay it and we could sort out the details later on. They refused. Said it was best I did buy it but just to go ahead and kit out my own room. When we went back to the house the daughter was waiting for us. It surprised me at the time yet it was the end of the month and she obviously had to have a key of her own. When I asked after the old woman she replied, Same as ever.

Is she comfortable? I said. It was daft to ask that but too late to retract. The daughter nodded without speaking and I noticed the other two exchanging grins. If they had been prepared to open their mouths then I wouldnt have had to say a word, but they always left me to sort out the business stuff. It was me who got this place. If I hadnt have made the phone call they would never have bothered. After she left with the rent money I told them I would be happy to stay in and watch the sport on television. Immediately Freddie jumped to his feet saying he fancied a pint and then Bob was on his feet saying, A good idea. Off they went, right away. That was definitely that. Something up, no doubt about it. Neither had even given me the opportunity of refusing. Yet I might not have refused. How could they know without even asking? It was as if they were waiting for me to say what I was going to do just so they could go and do something else. They lacked the nerve to come right out with it though. And when they suggested a game of cards later in the day I said no. Bob muttered something about where was I going, was I going out or what? I shrugged. Ten minutes later I went out. To hell with them.

The place was in darkness when I came home. A bit eerie in some ways. I walked along the hallway and flung open the lounge door, but with too much force, and it rocked on its hinges. Of course the room was empty. They had probably gone out as soon as possible after me. I switched on the television and tried to concentrate on it. Past 11 o'clock. The pub was less than ten minutes away. Normally we would have returned by then. Perhaps they had gone to another pub. Yet surely they would have gone there knowing it was where I would have gone? I hadnt gone there of course, but they werent to know that.

I had decided to wait up for them. I changed my mind. Why bother? They could have gone anywhere, they could have gone into the centre of town. Maybe even gone to the dancing somewhere. Why had they not even thought to mention it earlier? They could have said something. And if they hadnt truly known at that time they could at least have mentioned probabilities. If I had known they might be considering the dancing I would have gone out with them. Anywhere at all for that matter as long as it wasnt to the local pubs. Obviously my company was being avoided. And the way my suggestions were never picked up. They said there was no problem about sleeping. Neither there was, for them. Sleeping downstairs on a thick carpet! What's up? did they lack the guts to sleep in empty rooms!

No point staying up any longer. I switched off the television, the light too. Then in the hallway I couldnt find the switch for the light there. Not that it mattered because of the moonlight coming through the window on the first landing upstairs. Why had the old woman insisted on locking that door downstairs though? It was a question the three of us had discussed on a few occasions. Just as I approached my room I heard noises from outside. It was those two. Then the door had opened. They walked inside, the door closing as if they had only thrown it back instead of actually shutting it properly. They went into the lounge, one of them laughed at something the other must have said.

Yet the following morning was good! Freddie cooked a great breakfast. The first genuine meal we had prepared on the oven. From then on it was agreed we would eat as often as possible in the house and save on the money. I suggested we take turn about with the different things but Bob said since Freddie's cooking was fine he should stick to that and we could do the other bits if it was okay with everybody? Freddie agreed right away so I cut the cards with Bob. I lost. But fortunately he preferred to dry the dishes rather than wash them. I prefer the washing because it gets it over and done with. So it all worked out fine. The early part of the evening we went to the local but they agreed almost immediately when I suggested going into the town. Back home they preferred watching television to setting up a game of cards. By the time Bob came back from what seemed like his daily bath the credits for the late night movie were just coming on. I was lighting a cigarette and getting ready to settle down for it but then he made a display of unrolling the sleeping bag and generally busying about the place. I ignored it. But Freddie was wanting to know if he was getting ready for a kip? Yes, he said. To be fresh for work in the morning, apparently. I kept staring at the screen. He yawned and got into the sleeping bag. Silence for maybe five minutes then Freddie also yawned, a really big one. I got up and left. It was pointless.

My own sleeping bag was lying as I had left it that morning. In the corner was the pile of socks and stuff I had ready for the launderette. I would go straight from work tomorrow. Also I decided to buy a carpet right away. In fact a bed would be better. Why not? With the money a carpet cost it would probably be just the same to get a secondhand bed. I could even buy both. Without bothering about those two downstairs. Why should I? They could look after themselves. And I was sick of making decisions anyway. They never had a clue about that kind of thing. Even this area of the city was unknown to them. They would have had no chance of getting a place on their own,

without me. Why on earth did they go to bed when a good film
was starting? Why not. The lounge was perfect for a good
genuine sleep with that carpet blocking out the cold hard floor.
Bastards. Things would have to change otherwise. What?
Otherwise what! It was my place. It was me found the house. It
was me had to convince them it was great value, that it wasnt
too good to be true — that it was at least worth the price of a
phone-call!

I picked an old newspaper from the floor and wedged it
beneath the door to secure it and combat the draught.
Whenever I forgot this it banged all night — gently right
enough, but a bang nevertheless, especially when you are trying
to get a decent sleep. And also the bits of fluff and oose, they
would go breezing about the linoleum, and occasionally I felt as
if it was landing on my face, getting into my hair — that's the
trouble with sleeping on the floor. I laid my shoes on the
newspaper to secure it. There was no question that a good
carpet was the first necessity.

I was hardly sleeping at all now and my timekeeping was
beginning to suffer. Occasionally I worked a little overtime to
compensate but this day I returned home to find the old
woman's specially locked door lying ajar. An ancient sort of
smell hung everywhere. A kind of storeroom it looked like,
furniture stacked against walls, faded photographs in frames. If
the daughter discovered what had happened she would be well
within her rights to order us out at once. Why had they done it?
They never thought. How could the lock be fixed? It had
obviously been forced. How could everything be put right so
she would never notice? The kind of questions that never
seemed to occur to those two. I went upstairs immediately and
attempted to concentrate on a book. It was hard going. It
seemed like hours until at last the outside door opened. When
the lounge door closed I rose quietly and switched off my room
light, muffling the click by holding a sock over the switch. I
wanted them to think I had been asleep for ages. Back in the
sleeping bag I lay awake for a long time, just listening, but not

hearing anything unusual. What maybe I should have done earlier was to go right into the lounge and see what was going on. But what would've happened if they had found me there? Nothing. It was the lounge. I had as much right to be there as they had. Because they slept in the room didnt mean it wasnt a lounge. But what was going to happen about the old woman's room? Surely they hadnt searched the place? What would there be to find? It was just a kind of storeroom!

They admitted breaking into the old woman's room. Purely out of curiosity. They said they had taken nothing whatsoever, and hardly glanced at what was there. And promised to have it fixed by the Saturday in case the daughter arrived. Yet I doubt whether they would have spoken about it unless I had broached the subject. They showed no interest in the door to my room. It had blown open the night before. A gale was blowing outside and this might have been the cause. It seemed unlikely at the time and no more so now, possible of course, but just unlikely. It was pointless talking about it to them. As I lay soaking in the bathtub the cupboard door squeaked as usual, revealing the felt round the boiler. And what seemed to be a black hat perched on top, on the spot it would have been had the boiler been a body. I slid under the warm water, enjoying the sensation, but then I came up. Surely it was a hat! And coupled with the felt it really did resemble a body. It might have been a wrapped up towel made to look like a hat. It was definitely a hat. I got out the bath and strode across to open the door fully. It was a hat of course, perched on the top by having been balanced against the back pipe. And who had done the balancing? Some joke. Let's have a big laugh.

I dried. Maybe they were expecting a scream! I rushed down stairs and grasped the handle of their door but paused, just to control my anger. The light was out when I entered. Bob had sat up straight, he showed relief to see it was me. He muttered something, not loudly enough to waken Freddie who seemed to be sleeping. Their sleeping bags lay end to end in front of the fireplace. I wanted to know who put the hat on the boiler? I asked him again. Still he didnt answer. I shook my head. It was pointless. Outside in the hallway I paused again, wondering if I should stay there and find out if Freddie actually was asleep. But what difference did it make?

I stayed clear of them. That business about eating in had never taken on from the start. Humming and hawing about the time it took when you come back from working all day etc. Rubbish. The Saturday morning the daughter was certain to arrive for the rent I went down to wait but she never appeared. I saw Freddie through the open lounge door and he came out and asked if I was going out? Yes. Where? Ha ha ha. When will you be back? I told him I would be back eventually and let it hang as if I was going to be gone for the whole weekend or something. In fact I went up the town and intended going to a movie that evening, though I ended up in quite a good pub which had entertainment on Saturday nights. Once home I strolled along the path and stood at the door for a few moments then I opened it and strode down the hallway whistling, I had let the door shut itself by shoving it. I went straight into the lounge. They were watching television. I took out a can of beer and opened it, then I left. Loud noises woke me next morning.

It was midday by the time I went down. When I walked into the lounge the place was full of furnishings and fittings. A sideboard at one wall, a table near the window, some chairs. They were lying on the carpet reading the Sunday papers. Without saying anything I went out and along to the old woman's room. It had practically been cleared. What was the point.

They were standing in the doorway behind me. One of them indicated a couple of musty carpets and suggested I take them. The other said what about the big trunk in the corner, was that any good? Ha ha ha. I couldnt believe it. There could be no question that the daughter would notice next time she came. Freddie muttered something about sticking the stuff back in on the Friday night. What happened if she came unexpectedly? Well they could stick the stuff back in every Friday night to be on the safe side. Some idea that! What happens if she decided to look in on another day altogether, just to check up on us? Silence. They both shrugged. What about me? Oh great, two ancient carpets and a big trunk. Exactly what I need for the room!

Rubbish.

But the crux had taken place. This was it. The lounge was now theirs. It belonged to them. It didnt have anything to do with me. The television set and the orange carpet just happened to be in the room they now used as a bedsitter. I had the rest of the house. I could go anywhere I wanted. The only snag was there was nothing in it. Oh well, not much of a snag!

I went up the stairs and got ready to go out. That was it now. All the plans to decorate the place from top to bottom. All finished. And the garden. Getting the stuff growing properly, seeing the fruit would come out right. The whole lot. All finished. Yes, I could stay in an empty room and they would stay in the lounge. And we would all continue with an even three-way split of the rent. Yes. Fine! Exactly fair.

The door opening was becoming more frequent. It usually seemed to occur in the small hours. Then the silence. Because of the situation I was lying there anticipating anything. Anything at all. But I couldnt even hear their footsteps. It was possible they crept up to the attic to wait a while in case I got up to investigate. One morning I managed to get the early bus I told them people who went about pulling stunts in the middle of the night should be locked away in a kids' nursery. It was Freddie who spoke. He muttered something about my room, a smell. That was good. Freddie. As far as I knew he had never taken a bath since coming to the house! He showered in work, apparently. There was a smell in my room. I knew there was. I hadnt been to the launderette for a while. But I always opened the window for a bit during the early evening if I was home. The real smell belonged to the room itself. In fact the whole house had a smell of its own. Musty. I mentioned it to the daughter on that Saturday morning. Eventually she told me it was a while since it had been aired properly which was fair enough considering the way her mother was. It is doubtful whether she would have done it for years! The daughter picked up the rent envelope and left but I went down the path after her and asked if she had happened to take a look in the lounge recently. She said she was a bit pushed for time. I told her about the furniture. It was unintentional. It just came out. But she just said she was pushed for time again and that was that. I was glad but at the same time not glad. And then I saw she was gazing at the lounge window when she passed on the other side of the big scrawny hedge. Very possibly she would be back to check. And no wonder. Who wants strangers poking about in your mother's room? I had forgotten to mention the television set into the bargain. As far as I had been aware it was only in the house temporarily. Had the old woman not said both it and the orange carpet were going to be collected? What if she had forgotten about them? It could be she had. Being an old person she might well have remembered them but not known where they were. What would happen if it was a rented set? She might end up having to pay the full price as if she had had it stolen. Those rental firms are notorious. But the daughter would see it there in the lounge and know right away it was the one belonging to her mother. It would be fine.

I had to work part of Sunday because of this sleeping in. The man in charge was continually berating me about it and though he was justified to a large extent it was not as if I wasnt trying. At times it got so bad I would rather have taken the whole day off rather than go in and face it all. But I had to! What would have happened if I hadnt? There wasnt much could've happened. I could have been given the sack but I was good at my work. The man in charge obviously knew this. Where would they have got a better worker? Probably they could have — eventually, not right away. I didnt feel like going home when I got off the bus. It had been a long drawn out journey. Sunday bus services. I hardly had any energy left. I went to the chip shop and ate a meal, half expecting to see those two but they were probably off for the day somewhere, at least into the town.

I hadnt been to the local pub for some time. It was packed full when I got there and the way I was feeling I had to get a seat. I was obliged to sit at a table where a group of people were. They were regulars. Although I didnt know them well enough to talk to I didnt feel too much of an outsider. Later on I saw *them*. They were at the bar and looked to have been there for ages judging by the position they had towards the side of it. How could I have failed to spot them before? And how did they not see me? They maybe had and ignored me. It would have been unlikely they could have missed me. Normally when someone enters a pub the first thing is to gaze about for familiar faces. Habit. Everybody does it. If they hadnt been standing to the side I would definitely have seen them earlier. And they probably hadnt even been there when I arrived. What would they do if I ordered a drink at a place where they had to notice me? They could scarcely pretend not to see me — especially with the big mirror on the wall. The pub was busy but so what, they would still have to see me. What would happen? Would they buy me a drink? Ignore me? How could that happen! Impossible. That would be going too far. Even if they wanted to. And of course they would want to. But they couldnt. They werent in a position to. It would be a sort of confrontation. Right out in the open and in a public place. And what could they do? Nothing. Nothing whatsoever! There was nothing they could do except say hello or something, buy me a drink maybe and ask about my job. No chance of them doing anything else. And they could never force me into leaving the place. That was probably the real plan, get me to leave the house altogether. Ha ha ha. And if I hadnt phoned nobody would have. I saw Freddie exchange words with a person next to them at the bar there and they laughed briefly. It would remain to be seen. Things change. Because things are as they are it's no guarantee they have to stay like that. A very different story if I was to go up and start talking right now. Very different from two to one in the downstairs room. No pretences. Simple comments only. That'd be all. And they would have no option but to answer. What else could they do? They couldnt do

67

anything else. The barman happened along just then and he lifted my empty glass. I sat on for a moment. I could get myself another drink right now. What would happen? I didnt have to order at their side of the bar. If I did I would have to be ready. There was no point rushing in without having the thing prepared otherwise I couldnt keep the advantage. It had to be something direct. An opening comment to leave them floundering. Yet one more was also required in case they managed a quick reply. And it had to be short, brief. It was necessary to think things out. I left quickly but waited outside on the pavement for a moment. No, it would have been pointless at this stage. It had to be right. No sense to go rushing in and blabbing something. It had to be that nothing more could be said after such a confrontation — otherwise what was the point? No, time spent on details would not be wasted. I wondered if they had seen me leave but this was unlikely. I strode home as quickly as possible and went straight into their room and folded up their sleeping bags, I stuck them into the boiler cupboard in the bathroom. Then I got their shaving stuff and stuck it inside beside them. But it was too much. It was ridiculous. What would happen when they found it there? They might not find it at all. Of course they would. They would search the house. They would find it. What would they do? They would know who was responsible right away. What did it matter? It didnt matter. I left it all there. Another idea. I got a chair from their room and took it to behind the staircase to climb onto, to switch off the electricity at the mains. I stuck the chair back in the room and left the house. I went back to the chip shop and sat in the eating-inside area. But it was daft. Who else could have done it? There was nobody else. They would know who was responsible right away. Of course they would and I could just deny it. What could they do? Nothing. There was nothing they could do! All they could do was say, It was you! Ha ha ha. I ordered something to eat. It wasnt as if it was anything bad. Irritating at first but it would all be found. Maybe it already was. In fact it might well have been. They didnt like staying out too late to do a thing even if I'd wanted to.

They could have found the stuff and be sound asleep at this very minute. It would have surprised them and they would know who was responsible but so what, this was the best thing about it. Enough to let them see how things shift. I strolled about before going home at last. Maybe I shouldnt have tampered with their belongings. So far they hadnt actually done that to me. Yet compared to other things it was really nothing. If it upset them what on earth would they have done if their door had been kicked open in the early hours of a working morning? Even the hat!

The place was in darkness. Inside I crept up the stairs and undressed as quietly as I possibly could. I decided against using the bathroom until much later when it was certain they would be in and sleeping. But they would be in. It had to be after midnight. I listened. I heard nothing unusual. I continued to listen and then on impulse I got out the sleeping bag and used a sock to muffle the click of the light switch. The light came on. I switched it off.

That was that!

They had missed the bus next morning. When I passed along the hallway they appeared from the room. It was unexpected but I didnt find it totally surprising. Bob muttered something about having read any meters lately? I walked on. They spoke to each other. I could feel the anger getting up in me. I was about shaking. It was coming to the head. But it was the wrong time. I wasnt ready. I turned and stared at them. I didnt speak, I just looked. Then I went out. And even if I had been prepared it would have been pointless. Very different in a place like the public bar of a local pub. That would have been a real confrontation. Yet even then I would have to see everything was right, prepared.

The man in charge was at the window of the office when I arrived. I didnt want to go in. I wanted to get back to the house. It was pointless not to.

Everything was neat in the room. Their sleeping bags were

folded, one lying on a chair and one lying on the big trunk. A poster covered the blank spot above the mantelpiece. But if the old woman's stuff had been shoved back into her room what would be left? Nothing. Sleeping bags and a poster you could buy anywhere. I lit a cigarette. Then all of the furniture including the television set and the orange carpet I carted straight through into the old woman's place. I could close the door but not lock it. How did they do it? Maybe they didnt even lock it at all! Maybe they just stuck the stuff back and hoped the daughter wouldnt check to see if the actual door had been broken open! I stayed in the house until an hour before they were due off the bus. I didnt come back until much later. Of course they would have known. Who cares? But the daughter could have done it. She could have come in unexpectedly to check in the lounge. And how could she be asked to stand by and let her mother's belongings be used by a couple of strangers? And what about the television and carpet? She had every right to take them as well. They didnt belong to them. They were only temporary. I had as much right to them as they did. In some respects even more. Turn and turn about. They had their turn and surely I should have mine. My room would have been a great place with a carpet and a television set. Even just to have borrowed them once or twice. We could've cut the cards to set the nights. Everybody would've wanted Saturday but it could've been worked out fairly.

The front door had slammed. When I got to the window I saw them disappear along the street.

A padlock had been fixed onto their door. It was brand new. I hadnt heard it being put on. They must have done the job while I was out and I missed seeing it when I came back. Why did they do it? They didnt have to. They could've let things come to a head and that could've been the confrontation. It would've all been sorted out. They didnt even know for certain it was me. It was obvious. But it wasnt certain. It could easily have been the daughter. And she had every right to do it. They couldnt know for certain it was me. But what would happen if they did? Nothing. Nothing could actually happen. They would have to speak perhaps. And they would have to be speaking soon anyway because I hadnt left my share of the rent out at the weekend. It wasnt on purpose. I just overspent. My wages havent been too good recently. I only had enough for getting to work and getting by on food for the week. But if they wanted the lounge as a bedsitter an agreement had to be worked out. The television and the carpet could be sorted out side by side otherwise — what? Otherwise what?

The padlock was a problem. The only alternative to forcing it was to go in through the window but maybe the thing was bolted down. Knowing how the old woman had been this was very likely. I went into the kitchen and looked about and then I saw a metal rod near the sink. It was long and sturdy enough. But still the snags about after. What would happen after? Who cares. Nothing to worry about — after! The padlock glinted, sparkling new. I struck it over and over but it wouldnt give. I wedged in the rod to use it like a crowbar but this wasnt working right either and I began battering it again and again then wedging it again till finally it creaked and came away, the whole apparatus including the screwnails, bright and shiny new. I booted the door open. The orange carpet was back in position but the television wasnt. Neither was anything else. Not even the sleeping bags. What happened? Had they left it all in the old woman's room? Or packed up and left? Packed up and left maybe. They hadnt been carrying anything going down the street. They could have done it earlier on. I turned to leave and made out the big writing on the wall. HA HA HA, it said. I could check the other room or just go up the stair. It was cold in the hallway. And that musty smell.

Away in Airdrie

During the early hours of the morning the boy was awakened by wheezing, spluttering noises and the smell of a cigarette burning. The blankets hoisted up and the body rolled under, knocking him over onto his brother. And the feet were freezing, an icy draught seemed to come from them. Each time he woke from then on he could either smell the cigarette or see the sulphur head of the match flaring in the dark. When he opened his eyes for the final time the man was sitting up in bed and coughing out: Morning Danny boy, how's it going?

I knew it was you.

Aye, my feet I suppose. Run through and get me a drink of water son will you.

Uncle Archie could make people laugh at breakfast, even Danny's father — but still he had to go to work. He said, If you'd told me you were coming I could've made arrangements.

Ach, I was wanting to surprise yous all. Uncle Archie grinned: You'll be coming to the match afterwards though eh?

The father looked at him.

The boys're through at Airdrie the day.

Aw aye, aye. The father nodded, then he shrugged. If you'd told me earlier Archie — by the time I'm finished work and that . . .

Uncle Archie was smiling: Come on, long time since we went to a match the gether. And you're rare and handy for a train here as well.

Aye I know that but eh; the father hesitated. He glanced at

the other faces round the table. He said, Naw Archie. I'll have to be going to my work and that, the gaffer asked me in specially. And I dont like knocking him back, you know how it is.

Ach, come on—

Honest, and by the time I finish it'll be too late. Take the boys but. Danny — Danny'll go anywhere for a game.

Uncle Archie nodded for a moment. How about it lads?

Not me, replied Danny's brother. I've got to go up the town.

Well then . . . Uncle Archie paused and smiled: Me and you Danny boy, eh!

Aye Uncle Archie. Smashing.

Here! — I thought you played the game yourself on Saturdays?

No, the father said, I mean aye — but it's just the mornings he plays, eh Danny?

Aye. Aw that'll be great Uncle Archie. I've never been to Broomfield.

It's no a bad wee park.

Danny noticed his mother was looking across the table at his father while she rose to tidy away the breakfast stuff. He got up and went to collect his football gear from the room. The father also got up, he pulled on his working coat and picked his parcel of sandwiches from the top of the sideboard. When the mother returned from the kitchen he kissed her on the cheek and said he would be home about half past two, and added: See you when you get back Archie. Hope the game goes the right way.

No fear of that! We'll probably take five off them. Uncle Archie grinned, You'll be kicking yourself for no coming — best team we've had in years.

Ach well, Danny'll tell me all about it. Okay then . . . he turned to leave. Cheerio everybody.

The outside door closed. Uncle Archie remained by himself at the table. After a moment the mother brought him an ashtray and lifted the saucer he had been using in its stead. He said, Sorry Betty.

You're smoking too heavy.

I know. I'm trying to . . . He stopped; Danny had come in carrying a tin of black polish and a brush, his football-boots beneath his arm. As he laid the things in front of the fireplace he asked: You seen my jersey mum?

It's where it should be.

The bottom drawer?

She looked at him. He had sat down on the carpet and was taking the lid off the tin of black polish. She waited until he placed an old newspaper under the things, before leaving the room.

Hey Danny, called the Uncle. You needing any supporters this morning?

Supporters?

Aye, I'm a hell of a good shouter you know. Eh, wanting me along?

Well . . .

What's up? Uncle Archie grinned.

Glancing up from the book he was reading Danny's brother snorted: He doesnt play any good when people's watching.

Rubbish, cried Danny, it's not that at all. It's just that — the car Uncle Archie, see we go in the teacher's car and there's hardly any space.

With eleven players and the driver! Uncle Archie laughed: I'm no surprised.

But I'll be back in plenty of time for the match, he said as he began brushing the first boot.

Aye well you better because I'll be off my mark at half twelve pronto. Mind now.

Aye.

It's yes, said the mother while coming into the room, she was carrying two cups of fresh tea for herself and Uncle Archie.

Danny was a bit embarrassed, walking with his uncle along the road, and over the big hill leading out from the housing scheme, down towards the railway station in Old Drumchapel. But he met nobody. And there was nothing wrong with the scarf his uncle was wearing, it just looked strange at first, the blue and white, really different from the Rangers' blue. But supporters of a team were entitled to wear its colours. It was better once the train had stopped at Queen Street Station. Danny was surprised to see so many of them all getting on, and hearing their accents. In Airdrie Uncle Archie became surrounded by a big group of them, all laughing and joking. They were passing round a bottle and opening cans of beer.

Hey Danny boy come here a minute! Uncle Archie reached out to grip him by the shoulder, taking him into the middle of the group. See this yin, he was saying: He'll be playing for Rangers in next to no time . . . The men stared down at him. Aye, went on his uncle, scored two for the school this morning. Man of the Match.

That a fact son? called a man.

Danny reddened.

You're joking! cried Uncle Archie. Bloody ref chalked another three off him for offside! Eh Danny?

Danny was trying to free himself from the grip, to get out of the group.

Another man was chuckling: Ah well son you can forget all about the Rangers this afternoon.

Aye you'll be seeing a *team* the day, grunted an old man who was wearing a bunnet with blue and white checks.

Being in Broomfield Park reminded him of the few occasions he had been inside Hampden watching the Scottish Schoolboys. Hollow kind of air. People standing miles away could be heard talking to each other, the same with the actual players, you could hear them grunting and calling out names. There was a wee box of a Stand that looked like it was balancing on stilts.

The halftime score was one goal apiece. Uncle Archie brought him a bovril and a hot pie soaked in the watery brown sauce. A rare game son eh? he said.

Aye, and the best view I've ever had too.

Eat your pie.

The match had ended in a two all draw. As they left the

terracing he tagged along behind the group Uncle Archie was walking in. He hung about gazing into shop windows when the game was being discussed, not too far from the station. His uncle was very much involved in the chat and after a time he came to where Danny stood. Listen, he said, pointing across and along the road. See that cafe son? Eh, that cafe down there? Here, half a quid for you — away and buy yourself a drink of ginger and a bar of chocolate or something.

Danny nodded.

And I'll come and get you in a minute.

He took the money.

I'm just nipping in for a pint with the lads . . .

Have I to spend it all?

The lot. Uncle Archie grinned.

I'll get chips then, said Danny, but I'll go straight into the cafe and get a cup of tea after, okay?

Fair enough Danny boy fair enough. And I'll come and get you in fifteen minutes pronto. Mind and wait till I come now.

Danny nodded.

He was sitting with an empty cup for ages and the waitress was looking at him. She hovered about at his table till finally she snatched the cup out of his hands. So far he had spent twenty five pence and he was spending no more. The remaining money was for school through the week. Out from the cafe he crossed the road, along to the pub. Whenever the door opened he peered inside. Soon he could spot his uncle, sitting at a long table, surrounded by a lot of men from the match. But it was impossible to catch his attention, and each time he tried to keep the door open a man seated just inside was kicking it shut.

He wandered along to the station, and back again, continuing on in the opposite direction; he was careful to look round every so often. Then in the doorway of the close next to the pub he lowered himself to sit on his heels. But when the next man was entering the pub Danny was onto his feet and in behind him, keeping to the rear of the man's flapping coat tails.

You ready yet Uncle Archie?

Christ Almighty look who's here.

The woman's closing the cafe.

Uncle Archie had turned to the man sitting beside him: It's the brother's boy.

Aw, the man nodded.

What's up son?

It's shut, the cafe.

Just a tick, replied Uncle Archie. He lifted the small tumbler to his lips, indicated the pint glass of beer in front of him on the table. Soon as I finish that we'll be away son. Okay? I'll be out in a minute.

The foot had stretched out and booted the door shut behind him. He lowered himself onto his heels again. He was gazing at an empty cigarette packet, it was being turned in abrupt movements by the draught coming in the close. He wished he could get a pair of wide trousers. The mother and father were against them. He was lucky to get wearing long trousers at all. The father was having to wear short trousers and he was in his last year at school, just about ready to start serving his time at the trade. Boys nowadays were going to regret it for the rest of their days because they were being forced into long trousers before they needed to. Wide trousers. He wasnt bothered if he couldnt get the ones with the pockets down the sideseams, the ordinary ones would do.

The door of the pub swung open as a man came out and passed by the close. Danny was at the door. A hot draught of blue air and the smells of the drink, the whirr of the voices, reds and whites and blues and whites all laughing and swearing and chapping at dominoes.

He walked to the chip shop.

Ten number tens and a book of matches Mrs, for my da.

The woman gave him the cigarettes. When she gave his change he counted it slowly, he said: Much are your chips?

Same as the last time.

Will you give us a milky-way, he asked.

He ate half of the chocolate and covered the rest with the wrapping, stuck it into his pocket. He smoked a cigarette; he got to his feet when he had tossed it away down the close.

Edging the door ajar he could see Uncle Archie still at the table. The beer was the same size as the last time. The small tumbler was going back to his lips. Danny sidled his way into the pub, but once inside he went quickly to the long table. He was holding the torn-in-half tickets for the return journey home, clenched in his right hand. He barged a way in between two men and put one of the tickets down on the table quite near to the beer glass.

I'm away now Uncle Archie.

What's up Danny boy?

Nothing. I'm just away home . . . He turned to go then said loudly: But I'll no tell my mother.

He pushed out through the men. He had to get out. Uncle Archie called after him but on he strode sidestepping his way beyond the crowded bar area.

Twenty minutes before the train would leave. In the waiting room he sat by the door and watched for any sign of his uncle. It was quite quiet in the station, considering there had been a game during the afternoon. He found an empty section in a compartment of the train, closed the door and all of the windows, and opened the cigarette packet. The automatic doors shut. He stared back the way until the train had entered a bend in the track then stretched out, reaching his feet over onto the seat opposite. He closed his eyes. But had to open them immediately. He sat up straight, he dropped the cigarette on the floor and then lifted it up and opened the window to throw it out; he shut the window and sat down, resting his head on the back of the seat, he gazed at the floor. The train crashed on beneath the first bridge.

The chief thing about this game

McGraty had to wait outside the door for a while. Then the foreman called him in and explained the job he was putting him to work on. He took him to the machine and left him with the man there. Show him the ropes Tony, he added.

Tony glanced at McGraty. I thought they were sending a young fellow. I dont mean you're old or nothing.

McGraty shrugged.

Just stand and watch for the time being. And I might as well tell you, these shoes you're wearing, they're fucking hopeless. And the safety helmet. Surprised he allowed you in here without one.

Tony had picked up a pair of enormous heavy-duty clamps while he was speaking. He positioned himself at a point to the side of the machine. Over the top McGraty could see the head of another man bobbing about now and again.

A banging noise. Tony had crouched, staring into the machine. Slowly a copper bar of some 6 feet in length and 8 inches square issued out from between rollers. It was white hot. Tony caught the end of it in the clamps once enough of the copper bar was showing and he allowed it to come forwards until it appeared set to clatter to the floor. But it stopped at the edge with his weight balancing it from the protruding end. He lowered this end onto a small metal trolley he manoeuvred into position with his right foot. He moved backwards so that the bar came off the rollers and dropped. Still with the clamps on the end he pushed it forwards into a different part of the machine and soon the bar disappeared through other rollers. Stepping back and to his left a pace Tony wiped his brow with his sleeve. The copper bar now issued from a different pair of rollers; it was much longer and narrower, and a great deal less hot than before. He pushed it into another place; he exchanged his clamps for a lighter pair, and wiped his brow. He glanced at McGraty. The process was repeated. He glanced at McGraty who nodded.

The banging noise. Tony crouched nearer the machine, and turned his back to it with the clamps poised slightly above. He muttered, Watch this bit.

McGraty also crouched a little.

There was a gap the size of a mouse-hole about a foot above the metal plated floor. Suddenly a wire thrust its way out and was caught by Tony who had immediately begun trotting to the rhythm of its movement in the direction of a sort of kerb twelve yards off. The wire still issued from the rollers. Upon reaching the kerb he thrust the wire straight into a narrow tunnel through it, and jumped over the kerb with the momentum of his trot. The tunnel was angled so that the wire was coming out directly across to where another man was standing at a smaller machine some thirty yards away.

Tony had returned. He was smoking a cigarette. Barely glancing at McGraty he asked if he had ever done any work on a roller before. McGraty shook his head: I was in the building game.

Tony frowned.

I never said I had on the form. McGraty shrugged, They told me there was six weeks probation so it can be learned.

Aye . . . He put the cigarette in his mouth and collected the heavy-duty clamps. I'll let you have a go before tea-break. Where's your gloves by the way?

Gloves?

Jesus Christ.

They never said anything about it.

You cant expect to work the clamps without the fucking things. Tony shook his head and strode round the machine, out of sight; he came back with the man who worked the copper bar from the other side and motioned McGraty over. He said: Tell him what you've just told me. About the gloves and that.

McGraty shrugged.

And the helmet, tell him about the safety helmet.

They never said fuck all about it either. And the boots, nothing about them.

Aye you'll have to buy them, said the other man, cause they dont supply them. Get them out the First Aid room. They cost a few quid right enough, but it gets deducted every week, it's no too bad. And the boots're okay, eh Tony?

Aye, no bad.

Wear them to the fucking dancing if you like, grinned the man.

McGraty also smiled, and he took a half smoked cigarette from behind his ear and struck a match for it.

Okay, said Tony, time for another yin.

McGraty had frowned and taken the cigarette out of his mouth, he studied it: Tastes like sugar or something.

Tony had not heard, and the other man was already out of sight behind the machine. An overhead crane was arriving with another copper bar which was white hot, straight out of the furnace at the bottom end of the factory floor. McGraty took another drag on the cigarette then stubbed it out.

After tea-break Tony came with a pair of old gloves he had found; the stitching was out in places. He shrugged. All I could find. Sort it out with the gaffer when you see him next.

McGraty pulled them on without replying. He lifted the heavy-duty clamps and stood exactly where Tony had earlier. The banging. The copper bar showed. He got the clamps round its end and dragged it out to its other end. He stood for a moment, then Tony kicked the metal trolley towards him. He nodded, manoeuvring the trolley into position with his right foot and the copper bar dropped to it, the clamps fell out of his hands and the copper bar clattered onto the trolley, turning it over and bouncing once. McGraty and Tony had jumped clear. Tony looked at him. What did you let it drop for?

My fingers were fucking burning. Fucking gloves. McGraty shook his head.

Tony was walking out from the area, he cupped his hand round his mouth and shouted: Heh Shug, Shug. A lift. Heh.

Seconds later the overhead crane began moving, it made a rattling noise across the ceiling and the driver let the big hook down when it arrived. Using the clamps Tony got one end of the copper bar off the floor and kicked the hook round it. The crane raised it to sufficient height for the trolley to be pushed beneath, then the hook was withdrawn and the crane rattled back down to the furnace. Tony nodded to McGraty who stepped forwards and took the clamps, fixing them round the tip of the copper bar but as he was pushing it closer to the machine the toe of his right shoe nudged it and burst into flames. He screamed as he jumped back. He stubbed and scraped the shoe on the floor until the flames went out. Tony doused the smouldering part with water from a milk bottle. I told you about boots, he muttered.

The man from behind the machine was standing watching, he smiled and walked forwards saying, Fun and games eh!

Tony made no answer but passed him and called on the cranedriver to return. When the copper bar was back on the trolley the other man said, No use, too fucking cold.

Aw christ. Tony shook his head and lit a fresh cigarette.

Dont worry, said the man, we've got a learner remember. Just dock it off the timesheet.

Aye. Tony instructed the cranedriver and soon the copper bar was being returned to the furnace.

McGraty was leaning against the wall at the rear of the machine. The other man grinned: Hot in here eh? Come on, we'll have a fucking bevy . . . He waved him to follow. Round on his own side he brought a thick brown bottle out of a small metal cupboard and after swigging a mouthful handed it to Tony who also swigged from it before handing it to McGraty. Tony said: Just take a sip, it's concentrated stuff, replaces the sweat or some fucking thing.

Good with vodka, said the other. Bring in a bottle the morrow and we'll give it a buzz.

McGraty half smiled; he smelled it. Lime. He nodded and

sipped some, passed it back to the other man and pointed to his cigarette: This tastes like sugar.

Aye. Tony nodded, Well, ready for another crack at it?

McGraty looked at him.

The overhead crane was withdrawing a new copper bar from the furnace. The other man said, You'll be alright as long as you dont panic, that's the chief thing about this game.

I didnt fucking panic.

Fair enough. You're still best to dive right in but. Otherwise it can start building up in you.

Tony nodded. And the other man continued, I've seen a new guy do what you do and then no try it till later. By that time he was fucked, the nerve gone and that; you're best to give it a go the now instead of hanging about just thinking.

Aye, said Tony.

McGraty exhaled smoke, he shook his head. Naw, no me, no till I get the right gear.

The other two men exchanged glances. Tony muttered, Well you better go and tell the gaffer.

Just now?

Aye. Tony shrugged. No point standing watching me all day if you're no even going to attempt the thing.

If I had the right gear I would.

You better tell the gaffer.

Fine, suits me.

A woman was in the office; she had a bundle of papers under one arm and she was waiting for the gaffer to sign a form. McGraty stayed outside until she left. He chapped the door. He chapped again and entered immediately. The gaffer gazed up at him from his chair behind a desk. My shoes, said McGraty, they're hopeless. Look what happened to this yin . . . and he displayed the burnt toe. I need steel toe-caps.

The gaffer nodded.

Same with the gloves. Look at this . . . McGraty showed the burst seams: No good, these bars are red hot. I dont know how that guy, Tony — I dont know how he manages just with his hands. I mean christ sake, even with these . . . And the bloody heat, it's murder polis so it is.

The gaffer nodded. The First Aid. You get all the gloves and that down there. The boots too.

I've got boots in the house.

Have you?

Aye.

Well. Fine. Okay then . . . The gaffer glanced at a printed piece of paper before him.

Will I go to the First Aid or what?

For the gloves?

Aye. And the safety helmet, the guy told me I needed one.

Oh christ aye, aye. You've got to keep it on too. At all times. Mind and tell the rest of them to stick to that. Hell of a important. The fucking Safety Officer does his nut if he catches anybody without it. Naw, you'll have to mind and wear it, at all times.

McGraty nodded.

At the dinner-break he left the other men and went along to the canteen, finding a space beside a group from a different factory section. He took out his sandwiches, he had bought a cup of tea at the counter. One of the men began talking to him for a spell. Later he borrowed a *Daily Record* and when the man noticed he was reading the racing section he indicated a boy across at another table. The young yin, said the man, he carries a line to the betting shop if you're interested.

Good . . . McGraty nodded and resumed the study. When he was leaving he stopped by the table and scribbled the names of his horses on the back of an empty cigarette packet, and gave the boy 55 pence with it. It's a comedy bet son, you want me to write it for you?

The boy shrugged.

McGraty returned him the pencil.

I'll bring you the copy at the break later, whereabouts you working?

That machine with all the rollers.

What . . . The boy moved his chair out and looked down at McGraty's shoes, he grinned and called to the others at the table. Heh, it's the new guy from the roller!

The others got up to see McGraty's shoe. He smiled, Some fucking job eh?

They were amused. McGraty scratched his head.

A copper bar had just been delivered. McGraty was standing near the wall, watching Tony prepare to receive it through the rollers. The cranedriver shouted on him. When he walked beyond the machine the man said: Is it you's got the good start to your line?

What?

I heard you'd a good start to your line?

Me?

So I heard, 10's and 16's, your first two.

Is that right?

Aye, as far as I hear . . . The cranedriver pressed a button and his machine moved off, back down towards the furnace. McGraty gazed after it for a moment. From behind the roller the other man called, You've knocked it off eh?

McGraty shrugged, I'll believe it when I see it.

Ah they'll no con you. It'll be gen.

You sure?

Aye . . . The man stopped when the banging noise was heard. McGraty returned to the other side of the roller in time to see Tony thrusting the bar back inside. He took out a cigarette, he chuckled quietly, briefly; he flipped the match away and exhaled smoke, he watched Tony moving to the next position.

Remember Young Cecil

Young Cecil is medium sized and retired. For years he has been undisputed champion of our hall. Nowadays that is not saying much. This pitch has fallen from grace lately. John Moir who runs the place has started letting some of the punters rent a table Friday and Saturday nights to play Pontoons, and as an old head pointed out the other day: that is it for any place, never mind Porter's.

In Young Cecil's day it had one of the best reputations in Glasgow. Not for its decoration or the rest of it. But for all round ability Porter's regulars took some beating. Back in these days we won the 'City' eight years running with Young Cecil Number 1 and Wee Danny backing up at Number 2. You could have picked any four from ten to make up the rest of the team. Between the two of them they took the lot three years running; snooker singles and doubles, and billiards the same. You never saw that done very often.

To let you know just how good we were, John Moir's big brother Tam could not even get into the team except if we were short though John Moir would look at you as if you were daft if you said it out loud. He used to make out Tam, Young Cecil and Wee Danny were the big three. Nonsense. One or two of us had to put a stop to that. We would have done it a hell of a lot sooner if Wee Danny was still living because Young Cecil has a habit of not talking. All he does is smile. And that not very often either. I have seen Frankie Sweeney's boy come all the way down here just to say hello; and what does Young Cecil do but give him a nod and at the most a how's it going without even a name nor nothing. But that was always his way and Frankie Sweeney's boy still drops in once or twice yet. The big noises remember Cecil. And some of the young ones. Tam! — never mind John Moir — Young Cecil could have gave Tam forty and potting only yellows still won looking round. How far.

Nowadays he can hardly be annoyed even saying hello. But he was never ignorant. Always the same.

I mind the first time we clapped eyes on him. Years ago it was. In those days he used to play up the Y.M., but we knew about him. A hall's regulars kind of keep themselves to themselves and yet we had still heard of this young fellow that could handle a stick. And with a first name like Cecil nobody needed to know what his last one was. Wee Danny was the Number 1 at the time. It is not so good as all that being Number 1 cause you have got to hand out big starts otherwise you are lucky to get playing, never mind for a few bob — though there are always the one or two who do not bother about losing a couple of bob just so long as they get a game with you.

Wee Danny was about twenty seven or thirty in those days but no more than that. Well, this afternoon we were hanging around. None of us had a coin — at least not for playing with. During the week it was. One or two of us were knocking them about on Table 3, which has always been the table in Porter's. Even John Moir would not dream of letting anyone mess about on that one. There were maybe three other tables in use at the time but it was only mugs playing. Most of us were just chatting or studying form and sometimes one would carry a line up to Micky at the top of the street. And then the door opened and in comes this young fellow. He walks up and stands beside us for a wee while. Then: Anybody fancy a game? he says.

We all looks at one another but at Wee Danny in particular and then we bursts out laughing. None of you want a game then? he says.

Old Porter himself was running the place in those days. He was just leaning his elbows on the counter in his wee cubby-hole and sucking on that falling-to-bits pipe of his. But he was all eyes in case of bother.

For a couple of bob? says the young fellow.

Well we all stopped laughing right away. I do not think Wee Danny had been laughing at all; he was just sitting up on the ledge dangling his feet. It went quiet for a minute then Hector Parker steps forward and says that he would give the young fellow a game. Hector was playing 4 stick at that time and hitting not a bad ball. But the young fellow just looks him up and down. Hector was a big fat kind of fellow. No, says the young yin. And he looks round at the rest of us. But before he can open his mouth Wee Danny is off the ledge and smartly across.

You Young Cecil from the Y.M.?

Aye, says the young fellow.

Well I'm Danny Thompson. How much you wanting to play for?

Fiver.

Very good. Wee Danny turns and shouts: William . . .

Old Porter ducks beneath the counter right away and comes up with Danny's jar. He used to keep his money in a jam-jar in those days. And he had a good few quid in there at times. Right enough sometimes he had nothing.

Young Cecil took out two singles, a half quid and made the rest up with a pile of smash. He stuck it on the shade above Table 3 and Wee Danny done the same with his fiver. Old Porter went over to where the mugs were playing and told them to get a move on. One or two of us were a bit put out with Wee Danny because usually when there was a game on we could get into it ourselves for a couple of bob. Sometimes with the other fellow's cronies but if there was none of them Wee Danny maybe just covered the bet and let us make up the rest. Once or twice I have seen him skint and having to play a money game for us. And when he won we would chip in to give him a wage. Sometimes he liked the yellow stuff too much. When he got a right turn off he might go and you would be lucky to see him before he had bevied it all in; his money right enough. But he had to look to us a few times, a good few times — so you might have thought: Okay I'll take three quid and let the lads get a bet with the deuce that's left . . .

But no. You were never too sure where you stood with the wee man. I have seen him giving some poor bastard a right sherricking for nothing any of us knew about. Aye, more than once. Not everybody liked him.

Meanwhile we were all settled along the ledge. Old Porter and Hector were applying the brush and the stone; Wee Danny was fiddling about with his cue. But Young Cecil just hung around looking at the photos and the shield and that, that Old Porter had on full view on the wall behind his counter. When the table was finally finished Old Porter began grumbling under his breath and goes over to the mugs who had still not ended their game. He tells them to fuck off and take up bools or something and locks the door after them. Back into his cubby-hole he went for his chair so he could have a sit-down to watch the game.

Hector was marking the board. He chips the coin. Young Cecil calls it and breaks without a word. Well, maybe he was a bit nervous, I do not know; but he made a right mess of it. His cue ball hit the blue after disturbing a good few reds out the pack on its way back up the table. Nobody could give the wee man a chance like that and expect him to stand back admiring the scenery. In he steps and bump bump bump — a break of fifty six. One of the best he had ever had.

It was out of three they were playing. Some of us were looking daggers at Danny, not every day you could get into a fiver bet. He broke for the next and left a good safety. But the young fellow had got over whatever it was, and his safety was always good. It was close but he took it. A rare game. Then he broke for the decider and this time it was no contest. I have seen him play as well but I do not remember him playing better all things considered. And he was barely turned twenty at the time. He went right to town and Wee Danny wound up chucking it on the colours, and you never saw that very often.

Out came the jam-jar and he says: Same again son?

Double or clear if you like, says Young Cecil.

Well Wee Danny never had the full tenner in his jar so he gives us the nod and in we dived to Old Porter for a couple of bob till broo day because to tell the truth we thought it was a bit of a flash-in-the-pan. And even yet when I think about it, you cannot blame us. These young fellows come and go. Even now. They do not change. Still think they are wide. Soon as they can pot a ball they are ready to hand out J.D. himself three blacks of a start. Throw their money at you. Usually we were there to take it, and we never had to call on Wee Danny much either. So how were we supposed to know it was going to be any different this time?

Hector racked them. Young Cecil won the toss again. He broke and this time left the cue ball nudging the green's arse. Perfect. Then on it was a procession. And he was not just a potter like most of these young ones. Course at the time it was his main thing just like the rest but the real difference was that Young Cecil never missed the easy pot. Never. He could take a chance like anybody else. But you never saw him miss the easy pot.

One or two of us had thought it might not be a flash-in-the-pan but had still fancied Wee Danny to do the business because whatever else he was he was a money-player. Some fellows are world beaters till there is a bet bigger than the price of renting the table then that is them — all fingers and thumbs and miscueing all over the shop. I have seen it many a time. And after Young Cecil had messed his break in that first frame we had seen Wee Danny do the 56 so we knew he was on form. Also, the old heads reckoned on the young fellow cracking up with the tenner bet plus the fact that the rest of us were into it as well. Because Wee Danny could pot a ball with a headcase at his back all ready to set about his skull with a hatchet if he missed. Nothing could put the wee man off his game.

But he met his match that day.

And he did not ask for another double or clear either. In fact a while after the event I heard he never even fancied himself for the second game — just felt he had to play it for some reason.

After that Young Cecil moved into Porter's, and ever since it has been home. Him and Wee Danny got on well enough but they were never close friends or anything like that. Outside they ran around in different crowds. There was an age gap between them right enough. That might have had something to do with it. And Cecil never went in for the bevy the way the wee man did. In some ways he was more into the game as well. He could work up an interest even when there was no money attached whereas Wee Danny was the other way.

Of course after Young Cecil met his he could hardly be bothered playing the game at all.

But that happened a while later — when we were having the long run in the 'City'. Cleaning up everywhere we were. And one or two of us were making a nice few bob on the side. Once Cecil arrived Wee Danny had moved down to Number 2 stick, and within a year or so people started hearing about Young Cecil. But even then Wee Danny was making a good few bob more than him because when he was skint the wee man used to run about different pitches and sometimes one or two of us went along with him and picked up a couple of bob here and there. Aye, and a few times he landed us in bother because in some of these places it made no difference Wee Danny was Wee Danny. In fact it usually made things worse once they found out. He was hell of a lucky not to get a right good hiding a couple of times. Him and Young Cecil never played each other again for serious money. Although sometimes they had an exhibition for maybe a nicker or so, to make it look good for the mugs. But they both knew who the 1 stick was and it never changed. That might have been another reason for them not being close friends or anything like that.

Around then Young Cecil started playing in a private club up the town where Wee Danny had played once or twice but not very often. This was McGinley's place. The big money used to change hands there. Frankie Sweeney was on his way up then and hung about the place with the Frenchman and one or two others. Young Cecil made his mark right away and a wee bit of a change came over him. But this was for the best as far as we were concerned because up till then he was just too quiet. Would not push himself or that. Then all of a sudden we did not have to tell him he was Young Cecil. He knew it himself. Not that he went about shouting it out because he never did that at any time. Not like some of them you see nicking about all gallus and sticking the chest out at you. Young Cecil was never like that and come to think about it neither was Wee Danny — though he always knew he was Wee Danny right enough. But now when Young Cecil talked to the one or two he did speak to it was him did the talking and we did not have to tell him.

Then I mind fine we were all sitting around having a couple of pints in the Crown and there at the other end of the bar was our 1 and 2 sticks. Now they had often had a drink together in the past but normally it was always in among other company. Never like this — by themselves right through till closing time. Something happened. Whenever Young Cecil went up McGinley's after that Wee Danny would be with him, as if he was partners or something. And they started winning a few quid. So did Sweeney and the Frenchman; they won a hell of a lot more. They were onto Young Cecil from the start.

Once or twice a couple of us got let into the club as well. McGinley's place was not like a hall. It was the basement of an office building up near George Square and it was a fair sized pitch though there was only the one table. It was set aside in a room by itself with plenty of seats round about it, some of them built up so that everybody could see. The other room was a big one and had a wee bar and a place for snacks and that, with some card tables dotted about; and there was a big table for Chemmy. None of your Pontoons up there. I heard talk about a speaker wired up for commentaries and betting shows and that from the tracks, but I never saw it myself. Right enough I was never there during the day. The snooker room was kept shut all the time except if they were playing or somebody was in cleaning the place. They kept it well.

McGinley and them used to bring players through from Edinburgh and one or two up from England to play exhibitions and sometimes they would set up a big match and the money changing hands was something to see. Young Cecil told us there was a couple of Glasgow fellows down there hardly anybody had heard about who could really handle a stick. It was a right eye-opener for him because up till then he had only heard about people like Joe Hutchinson and Simpson and one or two other who went in for the 'Scottish' regular, yet down in McGinley's there was two fellows playing who could hand out a start to the likes of Simpson. Any day of the week. It was just that about money-players and the rest.

So Young Cecil became a McGinley man and it was not long before he joined Jimmy Brown and Sandy from Dumfries in taking on the big sticks through from Edinburgh and England and that. Then Sweeney and the Frenchman set up a big match with Cecil and Jimmy Brown. And Cecil beat him. Beat him well. A couple of us got let in that night and we picked up a nice wage because Jimmy Brown had been around for a good while and had a fair support. In a way it was the same story as Cecil and Wee Danny, only this time Wee Danny and the rest of Porter's squad had our money down the right way and we were carrying a fair wad for some of us who were not let in. There was a good crowd watching because word travels, but it was not too bad; McGinley was hell of a strict about letting people in — in case too many would put the players off in any way. With just onlookers sitting on the seats and him and one or two others standing keeping an eye on things it usually went well and you did not see much funny business though you heard stories about a couple of people who had tried it on at one time or another. But if you ask me, any man who tried to pull a stroke down McGinley's place was needing his head examined.

Well, Young Cecil wound up the man in Glasgow they all had to beat, and it was a major upset when anybody did. Sometimes when the likes of Hutchinson came through we saw a fair battle but when the big money was being laid it was never on him if he was meeting Young Cecil. Trouble was you could hardly get a bet on Cecil less he was handing out starts. And then it was never easy to find a punter, and even when you did find one there was liable to be upsets because of the handicapping.

But it was good at that time. Porter's was always buzzing cause Young Cecil still played 1 stick for us with Wee Danny backing him up at Number 2. It was rare walking into an away game knowing everybody was waiting for Young Cecil and Porter's to arrive and the bevy used to flow. They were good days and one or two of us could have afforded to let our broo money lie over a week if we had wanted though none of us ever did. Obviously. Down in McGinley's we were seeing some rare tussles; Young Cecil was not always involved but since he was Number 1 more often than not he was in there somewhere at the wind up.

It went well for a hell of a long while.

Then word went the rounds that McGinley and Sweeney were bringing up Cuddihy. He was known as the County Durham at that time. Well, nobody could wait for the day. It was not often you got the chance to see Cuddihy in action and when you did it was worth going a long way to see. He liked a punt and you want to see some of the bets he used to make at times — on individual shots and the rest of it. He might be about to attempt a long hard pot and then just before he lets fly he stands back from the table and cries: Okay. Who'll lay me six to four to a couple of quid?

And sometimes a mug would maybe lay him thirty quid to twenty. That is right, that was his style. A bit gallus but he was pure class. And he could take a drink. To be honest, even us in Porter's did not fancy Young Cecil for this one — and that includes Wee Danny. They said the County Durham was second only to the J.D. fellow though I never heard of them meeting seriously together. But I do not go along with them that said the J.D. fellow would have turned out second best if they had. But we will never know.

They were saying it would be the best game ever seen in Glasgow and that is something. All the daft rumours about it being staged at a football ground were going the rounds. That was nonsense. McGinley was a shrewdie and if he wanted he could have put it on at the Kelvin Hall or something, but the game took place in his club and as far as everybody was concerned that was the way it should be even though most of us from Porter's could not get in to see it at the death.

When the night finally arrived it was like an Old Firm game on New Year's Day. More people were in the card-room than acutally let in to see the game and in a way it was not right for some of the ones left out were McGinley regulars and they had been turned away to let in people we had never clapped eyes on before. And some of us were not even let in to the place at all. Right enough a few of us had never been inside McGinley's before, just went to Porter's and thought that would do. So they could not grumble. But the one or two of us who would have been down McGinley's every night of the week if they had let us were classed as I do not know what and not let over the doorstep. That was definitely not fair. Even Wee Danny was lucky to get watching as he told us afterwards. He was carrying our money. And there was some size of a wad there.

Everybody who ever set foot in Porter's was onto Young Cecil that night. And some from down our way who had never set foot in a snooker hall in their lives were onto him as well, and you cannot blame them. The pawn shops ran riot. Everything hockable was hocked. We all went daft. But there was no panic about not finding a punter because everybody knew that Cuddihy would back himself right down to his last penny. A hell of a man. Aye, and he was worth a good few quid too. Wee Danny told us that just before the marker tossed the coin Cuddihy stepped back and shouts: Anybody still wanting a bet now's the time!

And there were still takers at that minute.

All right. We all knew how good the County Durham was; but it made no difference because everybody thought he had made a right bloomer. Like Young Cecil said to us when the news broke a week before the contest: Nobody, he says, can give me that sort of start. I mean it. Not even J.D. himself.

And we believed him. We agreed with him. It was impossible. No man alive could give Young Cecil thirty of a start in each of a five-frame match. It was nonsense. Wee Danny was the same.

Off of thirty I'd play him for everything I've got. I'd lay my weans on it. No danger, he says: Cuddihy's coming the cunt with us. Young Cecil'll sort him out proper. No danger!

And this was the way of it as far as the rest of us were concerned. Right enough on the day you got a few who bet the County Durham. Maybe they had seen him play and that, or heard about him and the rest of it. But reputations are made to be broke and apart from that few, Cuddihy and his mates, everybody else was onto Young Cecil. And they thought they were stonewall certainties.

How wrong we all were.

But what can you say? Young Cecil played well. After the event he said he could not have played better. Just that the County Durham was in a different class. His exact words. What a turn-up for the books. Cuddihy won the first two frames then Young Cecil got his chance in the next but Cuddihy came again and took the fourth for the best of five.

Easy. Easy easy.

What can you do? Wee Danny told us the Frenchman had called Cecil a good handicapper and nothing else.

Well, that was that and a hell of a lot of long faces were going about our side of the river — Porter's was like a cemetery for ages after it. Some of the old heads say it's been going downhill ever since. I do not know. Young Cecil was the best we ever had. Old Porter said there was none better in his day either. So, what do you do? Sweeney told Young Cecil it was no good comparing himself with the likes of Cuddihy but you could see it did not matter.

Young Cecil changed overnight. He got married just before the game anyway and so what with that and the rest of it he dropped out of things. He went on playing 1 stick for us for a while and still had the odd game down McGinley's once or twice. But slowly and surely he just stopped and then somebody spoke for him in Fairfield's and he wound up getting a start in there as a docker or something. But after he retired he started coming in again. Usually he plays billiards nowadays with the one or two of us that are still going about.

Mind you he is still awful good.

The habits of rats

This part of the factory had always been full of rats. It was the storeroom. Large piles of boxes were stacked at the bottom end while scattered about the floor was all manner of junk. Here in particular dwelled the rats. They came out at night. During the nightshift one man had charge of the storeroom; he was always pleased when somebody called up with an order and stayed for a chat. His office lay at the opposite end of the storeroom. He would keep all the lights on here but leave the bottom end in darkness, unless being obliged to go down to collect a box from stock, in which case he switched on every light in the entire place to advise the rats of his approach.

One night a gaffer phoned him on the intercom and told him to get such and such a box and deliver it immediately to the machineshop. Now the storeman had been halfway through the first of his cheese sandwiches at the time but the interruption did not annoy him. There was little work to keep his mind occupied during the night; he was always glad of the opportunity to wander round the factory pushing his wheelbarrow.

Once he had all the lights on at the bottom end he found himself to be holding his parcel of cheese sandwiches. Stuffing the remainder of the one he had been eating straight into his mouth he laid the parcel down on a box so that he could manoeuvre the requisitioned box onto the wheelbarrow. He pushed it along to the exit. He switched off the lights as he went. Outside the storeroom he halted. He dashed back inside and switched them on again and quickly went down to retrieve the

97

sandwiches before the rats could gobble them all up. In his office he placed the parcel on top of a filing cabinet.

He enjoyed the wander, stopping off here and there for a smoke or a chat with particular people he was friendly with. Back in the storeroom he brewed a fresh pot of tea and sat down to continue his lunchbreak. He only ate two of the sandwiches.

Later on in the night a gaffer phoned him with another requisition. He phoned back after when again there was no reply. Eventually he came round in person, to discover the storeman lying on the floor in a coma. He had the storeman rushed off to hospital at once.

For a fortnight the storeman remained in this coma. They took out all of his blood and filled him up with other blood. They said that a rat, or rats, had urinated on his sandwiches and thus had his entire blood system been poisoned.

The storeman said he could remember a slight dampness about the sandwiches he had eaten, but that they had definitely not been soggy. He reckoned the warmth of his office may have dried them out a bit. He said when he left them lying on the box he must have forgotten to close the parcel properly. But he was only gone moments. He could not understand it at all. After his period of convalescence they transferred him to a permanent job on the dayshift, across in the machineshop.

The block

The body landed at my feet. A short man with stumpy legs. He was staring up at me but though so wide open those eyes were seeing things from which I was excluded, not only excluded from but irrelevant to; things to which I was nonexistent. He had no knowledge of me, had never had occasion to be aware of me. He did not see me although I was staring at him through his eyeballs. I was possibly seeking some sort of reflection. What the hell was he seeing with his eyelids so widely parted. He was seeing nothing. Blood issued from his mouth. He was dead. A dead man on the pavement beneath me — with stumpy legs; a short man with a longish body. I felt his pulse: there was no pulse. I wasnt feeling his pulse at all. I was grasping the wrist of a short man. No longer a wrist. I was grasping an extension, the extension to the left of a block of matter. This block of matter was a man's body several moments earlier. Unless he had been dead on leaving the window upstairs, in which case a block of matter landed at my feet and I could scarcely even be referred to in connection with 'it', with a block of matter describable as 'it' — never mind being nonexistent of, or to. And two policemen had arrived. O Jesus, said one, is he dead?

I was looking at them. The other policeman had knelt to examine the block and was saying: No pulse. Dead. No doubt about it poor bastard. What happened? he addressed me.

A block of matter landed at my feet.

What was that?

The block of matter, it was a man's body previous to impact

unless of course he was out the game prior to that, in which case, in which case a block of matter landed at my feet.

What happened?

This, I said and gestured at the block. This; it was suddenly by my feet. I stared into the objects that had formerly been eyes before doing as you did, I grasped the left extension there to . . . see.

What?

The pulse. You were saying there was no pulse, but in a sense — well, right enough I suppose you were quite correct to say there was no pulse. I had grasped what I took to be a wrist to find I was grasping the left extension of a block of matter. Just before you arrived. I found that what was a man's body was in fact a block and

. . . do you live around here?

What, aye, yes. Along the road a bit.

Did you see him falling?

An impossibility.

He was here when you got here?

No. He may have been. He might well have been alive, it I mean. No — he . . . unless of course the . . . I had taken it for granted that it landed when I arrived but it might possibly . . . no, definitely not. I heard the thump. The impact. Of the impact.

Jesus Christ.

The other policeman glanced at him and then at me: What's your name?

McLeish, Michael. I live along the road a bit.

Where exactly?

Number 3.

And where might you be going at this time of the morning?

Work, I'm going to work. I'm a milkman.

The other policeman began rifling through the garments covering the block. And he brought out a wallet and peered into its contents. Robert McKillop, he said, I think his name's Robert McKillop. I better go up to his house Geordie, you stay here with . . . He indicated me in a vaguely surreptitious manner.

I'm going to my work, I said.

Whereabouts?

Partick.

The milk depot?

Aye, yes.

I know it well. But you better just wait here a minute.

The policeman named Geordie leaned against the tenement wall while his mate walked into the close. When he had reappeared he said, Mrs McKillop's upset — I'll stay with her meantime Geordie, you better report right away.

What about this yin here? I mean we know where he works and that.

Aye . . . the other one nodded at me: On your way. You'll be hearing from us shortly.

At the milk depot I was involved in the stacking of crates of milk onto my lorry. One of the crates fell. Broken glass and milk sloshing about on the floor. The gaffer swore at me. You ya useless bastard: he shouted. Get your lorry loaded and get out of my sight.

I wiped my hands and handed in my notice. Right now, I said, I'm leaving right now.

What d'you mean you're leaving! Get that fucking wagon loaded and get on your way.

No, I'm not here now. I'm no longer . . . I cannot be said to be here as a driver of milk lorries any more. I've handed in my notice and wiped my hands off the whole carry on. Morning.

I walked to the exit. The gaffer coming after me. McArra the checkerman had stopped singing and was gazing at us from behind a row of crates but I could see the cavity between his lips. The gaffer's hand had grasped my elbow. Listen McLeish, he was saying. You've got a job to do. A week's notice you have to give. Dont think you can just say you're leaving and then walk out the fucking door.

I am not here now. I am presently walking out the fucking door.

Stop when I'm talking to you!

No. A block of matter landed at my feet an hour ago. I have to be elsewhere. I have to be going now to be elsewhere. Morning.

Fuck you then. Aye, and dont ever show your face back in this depot again. McArra you're a witness to this! he's walking off the job.

Cheerio McArra. I called: I am, to be going.

Cheerio McLeish, said the checkerman.

Outside in the street I had to stop. This was not an ordinary kind of carry on. I had to lean against the wall. I closed my eyelids but it was worse. Spinning into a hundred miles of a distance, this speck. Speck. This big cavity I was inside of and also enclosing and when the eyelids had opened something had been presupposed by something. Thank Christ for that, I said, for that, the something.

Are you alright son?

Me . . . I . . . I was . . . I glanced to the side and there was this middle-aged woman standing in a dark coloured raincoat, in a pair of white shoes; a striped headscarf wrapped about her head. And a big pair of glasses, spectacles. She was squinting at me. Dizzy, I said to her, a bit dizzy Mrs — I'm no a drunk man or anything.

O I didnt think you were son I didnt think you were, else I wouldnt've stopped. I'm out for my messages.

I looked at her. I said: Too early for messages, no shops open for another couple of hours.

Aye son. But I cant do without a drop of milk in my tea and there was none left when I looked in the cupboard, so here I am. I sometimes get a pint of milk straight from the depot if I'm up early. And I couldnt sleep last night.

First thing this morning you could've called me a milk man, I said while easing myself up from the wall.

O aye.

I nodded.

Will you manage alright now?

Aye, thanks, cheerio Mrs.

Cheerio son.

I was home in my room. A tremendous thumping. I was lying face down on the bed. The thumping was happening to the door. McLeish. McLeish. Michael McLeish! A voice calling the name of me from outside of my room. And this tremendous thumping for the door and calling me by name McLeish! Jesus God.

Right you are, I shouted. And I pulled the pillow out from under my chin and pulled it down on the top of the back of my head. The thumping had stopped. I closed my eyelids. I got up after a second of that and opened the door.

We went to the depot, said one, but you'd left by then.

The second policeman was looking at my eyes. I shut the lids on him. I opened my mouth and said something to which neither answered. I repeated it but still no reply.

I told your gaffer what'd happened earlier on, said one. He said to tell you to give him a ring and things would be okay. No wonder you were upset. I told him that, the gaffer. Can we come in?

Can we come in? the other said.

Aye.

Can we come in a minute Michael? said the other.

I opened the door wider and returned to bed. They were standing at the foot of it with their hats in their hands. Then they were lighting cigarettes. A smoke, asked one. Want a smoke?

Aye. I'm not getting things out properly. I'm just not getting out it all the way. The block as well . . . it wasnt really the block.

Here . . . The other handed me an already burning cigarette.

I had it in my mouth. I was smoking. Fine as the smoke was entering my insides. The manner in which smoke enters an empty milk bottle and curls round the inner walls almost making this kind of shinnying noise while it is doing the curling. The other was saying: Nice place this. You've got some good pictures on the wall. I like that one there with the big circles. Is it an original?

Aye, yes. I painted it. I painted it in paint, the ordinary paint. Dulux I mean — that emulsion stuff.

Christ that's really good. I didnt know you were a painter.

It is good right enough, the other said.

Fingers. I used my pinkies; right and left for the adjacents. You know that way of touching the emulsion. That was what I was doing with the . . . I was . . . and the milk bottle, the milk bottle I suppose.

But dont let it get you down because the gaffer definitely did say you were to get in touch with him and it would be okay, about the job and that.

Aye, the other said. The thing is we'll need to go to the station. Our serjeant wants to hear how it happened with Mr McKillop this morning. How you saw it yourself — witnessed it Michael. We can get a refreshment down there, tea or coffee. Okay? — just shove on your clothes and we'll get going.

In the back seat of the patrol car one of them said: I'm not kidding but that painting of yours Michael, it was really good. Were the rest of them yours as well?

Aye, yes. I was doing painting. I was painting a lot sometimes. On the broo and that, before I started this job. In a sense though . . .

The policeman was looking at me, between my eyes; onto the bridge of my nose. I closed the eyelids: reddish grey. I could guess what would be going on. The whole of it. The description. A block of matter wasnt it. It would be no good for them — the serjeant, the details of it, the thump of impact. What I was doing and the rest of it. Jesus God. I was painting a lot sometimes, I said to him.

What's up?

Nothing. I'm just not getting the things, a hold . . . sploshing about.

It had to upset you — dont worry about that.

Not just the block but. Not just the block that I was . . . Ach.

I stopped and I was shaking my head. The words werent coming. Nothing at all to come and why the words were never. They cannot come by themselves. They can come by themselves. Without, not without. The anything. They can do it but only with it, the anything. What the fuck is the anything; that something. A particular set of things maybe.

Open the window a bit, the other said. Give him a breath of fresh air. Gets hell of a stuffy in here. And refreshments when we get there.

A wee room inside the station I was walked into. A policeman and a serjeant following. I was to sit at a table with the serjeant to be facing me. And he saying: I just want you to tell me what it was happened earlier on. In your own words Mr McLeish.

A block of matter, it was at my feet. I was . . . I glanced at the serjeant to add, I couldnt be said to be there in a sense. A thump of impact and the block of matter.

A block of matter, he replied after a moment. Yes I know what you're meaning about that. Mr McKillop was dead and so you didnt see him that way; you just saw him as a kind of shape — is that right, is that what you're meaning?

You could — I mean I could, be said to — no. No, I was walking and the thump, the block.

You were walking to work?

Aye, yes.

And the next thing, wham? the body lands at your feet?

No. In a sense though you . . . No, though; I was walking, thump, the block of matter. And yet — he was a short man, stumpy legs, longish body. And less then — less than, less than immediately a block of matter. Eyes. The objects that had been eyes. Jesus no. Not had been eyes at all. They were never eyes. Never ever had been eyes for the block. McKillop's eyes those objects had been part of. Part of the eyes. And I looked into them and they were not eyes. Just bits — bits of the block.

Look son I'm sorry, I know you're . . . The serjeant was glancing at the policeman. And his eyes!

Your gaze is quizzical: I said.

Ho. Quizzical is it!

Aye, yes.

And what is my gaze now then?

He was looking at me then I was looking out at him. He

began looking at the policeman. Without words, both talking away. I said, It doesnt matter anyhow.

What doesnt matter?

Nothing, the anything.

The serjeant stood up: I'll be back in a minute. He went out and came back in again carrying 3 cartons of tea and a folder under his arm. Tea Mr McLeish, he said, breaking and entering 1968, 69. But you said nothing about that though eh!

I grasped the carton of tea.

So, he continued while being seated. Out walking at the crack of dawn and wham, a block called McKillop lands at your feet.

That'll do, I said.

What'll do?

The serjeant was staring at my nose. I could have put an index finger inside. He was speaking to me. It's okay son breaking and entering has nothing to do with it, I just thought I'd mention it. We're not thinking you were doing anything apart from going to your work. A bit early right enough but that's when milk men go about. Mrs McKillop told us her end and you're fine.

Serjeant?

What?

Nothing.

After a moment he nodded: Away you go home. It's our job to know you were done in 68 69. A boy then but and I can see you've changed. A long time ago and Geordie tells me you've a steady job now driving the milk lorries and you've a good hobby into the bargain so — you're fine. And I dont think we'll need to see you again. But if we do I'll send somebody round. Number 3 it is eh? Aye, right you are. The serjeant stood up again and said to the policeman: Let him finish his tea.

Okay serj.

Fine. Cheerio then son, he said to me.

Jim dandy

So grateful to awaken to morning, even seeing the state of the dump. Very early as usual after a drink the night before. Such an erection, the immediate need to urinate. Nothing at all in the house bar a scrimp of cheese whose wrapping paper alone turns me off. And black coffee it has to be. Huddled in front of the electric fire, the uncomfortable heat, my trouser cuffs hanging then burning my skin when I sit back. On the second smoke with the same coffee I feel better though it is possible she will die in childbirth and I to rear the kid by myself.

The newsagent has me stay for tea which we sip munching chocolate biscuits, she wanting to find out the latest information. But how will I manage to earn a living. How is it to be done. The child being taken away from me. Or me having to give it away.

Back upstairs with the morning paper and for some reason I brush my teeth and follow with a smooth shave — the Visiting. And I dress like that, then later have a bath in the public washhouse. And consider a haircut.

She is so pleased to see me: Looking so spruce. Proud of me in front of the other women. They see me as a man against their own. Maybe they dont. I nod to certain among them I recognise and also to the man three beds along who wants a boy definitely, if possible. Being told about the state of the dump cheers her up. She really wants to come home, I want that so much I dont speak. Neither of us thinks of returning a trio. On the bus home I think of that. And later I wander round to her mother's with the news and borrow two quid and my dinner. And a couple of pints with my father-in-law. She's a good lassie, he says to me, a bit like her maw in some ways but no too bad son. Always had her eye on you you know, even when yous were weans together. Aye, and me going to be a granpa as well.

Me a father.

Aye. Jesus Christ. Hey Bertie, stick us a couple of Castellas eh. Aye and listen son, dont let her maw upset you. She likes you well enough.

I know that.

Aye. Aye, well. All the best son, cheers . . . And he gives me a fiver when we split, pushing it into the top pocket of my jacket, embarrassed. Claps me on the shoulder. He likes me okay and I like him and the mother-in-law is alright. He knows that because me and his daughter share the same bed sex has to happen. Maybe he regrets all the dirty jokes with his workmates or something.

Back at the hospital nothing is doing. The feeling that they were all enjoying the female banter before us crowd showed up. The looks from the staff. I am too sensitive. They arent really men haters. If you see what they have to see and so on. My aggression just. I shake her hand to leave but she gets me awake by demanding a kiss, it brings us together. Her smell. She hates to see me walking out of the place and when I get to the door I glimpse her, small there, watching me go. Fuck it. The protective male. Is what sickens the nurses maybe. Apart from me. It is just a fact. I cannot change, all that much.

In the local hangout a cloistered male group backs onto me with the stupid jokes and the new office girls and their quick glances at the door each time it bangs open. And the girl in the mirror ordering 2 shandies. Hell of a crush, I gasp to her. She half smiles as a reply. My stupid face in the mirror. I have to get out of this bar and Subway to the Cross. Quite a while since last

I was down here but the crowd are glad to see me and I explain the situation and drinks are going to get shoved in front of me I'm well aware. Soon drunk and the bouts of gabbing followed by blank silences.

On the road to somebody's home I let my legs wobble, confide to him supporting me that it's like this man, though I know it comes to everybody all the time I cant fucking help . . . The bastards in their spikinspan clothes. The shit in the back close. The yellow shades of newspaper hanging out the dustbin. The smelly black stuff puddling between the midden and the back close with bits of I dont know what floating about and the dog gangs following the bitch in their maze. The wean. And

But later I feel better — even to bawling, Dont worry about me, jim dandy, just what the doctor etceterad . . . When I overheard someone saying they should not have brought me.

The wives and the girlfriends. I slump in a chair glad to be breathing, to begin a conversation now and then. I am more acceptable, now known as married and expecting our first at that very minute. Yes. Everything's fine. So so. Cant complain and musnt bla. Course I want a dance. Feet still as fast as fuck — sorry. The girl dancing to me asks how I am doing and how it feels to be a daddy shortly and I wink. I wink. Jesus Christ. But she is there to make me enjoy being. Understands all. I see it. The Mother Earth. Someone's wife. Frank's wife. The old mate Frank. I spot him seated and chatting to a young thing — I followed my partner's eyes. And I cant be bothered at all. Everybody on the floor jumping up and down but me now, and some other girl, half hoping by the looks of things. I'm useless but, useless. I just want to be in this comfy chair wallowing and possibly getting to the stupor.

Somebody at my elbow poking me, to join in, Annie the wife of old mate Frank once again, tugging me by the arm: Come on — we're expecting a song from you in a minute.

Jesus. I hear big John singing the Green Grass of Home and everybody silent. The old hometown looks the same. Aye John. Give it laldy. The big John fellow giving it the big licks. Aye John, go on my son. And I am onto my feet and into the chorus with him. And when we finish a big round of applause when I jump to my feet once more but; Just a minute, I tell them, Back in a flash, desperately needing a jack dash.

I close the door. Out and along the road, up the Kelvin Way through into the park, crunching along the low gravel path by the river. At the first tree everything erupts. Retching for ages almost dozing on my feet there vomit I know caking the shoes and trouser cuffs, staggering along. On the hill 3 wineys, 2 males and a female share a bottle, talking; their voices carry in the night still. And asked for a smoke, by a single man on a bench and I give him one which I have to light, his hands dirt lined, warm to the touch. He inhaled deeply: Stick with me big yin, I'll get us a few bob tomorrow.

Black coffee. The television late movie. Aware of the surroundings here I am very aware, myself here. Jesus; the sheets kicked down over my feet in the smelly bed. Yet not the reeling brain thanks to vomit. Good old vomit clears heads. Is my momma and poppa. Too late to go downstairs and find out from the neighbours if I am a daddy. A note would have been pushed through the letterbox anyway. The feet freezing. Lumpen balls. I am stretching beneath this sheet now pushing my legs down my shoulders back as far as they all can go.

I shall be awake all night.

Once dressed I dipped my head into a basin of the cold water. And again. Opening the eyelids under water pulling the skin back on the sockets so the water can enter my brain. And down and out the front close sprinting along the street watching for a taxi as I go and in luck. Yes. Minutes later knocking the door and explaining about the lack of cigarette machines in the immediate vicinity so my apologies but I'll be begging smokes for the rest of the night. Apparently I am very pale. I tell Frank in a whisper I've been spending the past while spewing the ring and that. Thought so, he says, but they'll still be wanting a song off you. He poured me some beer and went to sit by his wife. I remember Annie. All around now people just sitting in couples with the music controlled. Soon as I leave the singing and the dancing stops: I shouts: What's the story at all!

Aw jesus look who's back, laughs big John. He is either Annie's cousin or Frank's cousin. I used to know which I think. Somebody takes records off and puts others on, and slips off her shoes. And a couple of girls get up, dragging their men behind. The dancing resumes. Later on I sit beside the girl I have been dancing with mainly. Sue. I vaguely know her from somewhere. The dancing halts. The bottle is spinning for another song, everybody glass in hand enjoying it all. When my turn comes Sue rises and leaves the room. She stays away even after I have finished.

The old house is still standing. At intervals I start awake and refill my glass if necessary. Snuggling close in on the floor a couple barely moving just rocking back and forth as if dancing in slowmotion. Nobody sings. Frank and Annie, big John and his wife, have been chatting to me about life in general and why me and the wife arent appearing these days. Relieved when I decide to go home. In the bathroom more cold water, and Sue steps in front of me as I come out. I have to go ben see her things or something more records maybe, well okay. I think I might have dozed off on the lavatory seat. I have a drink in my hand. And beside her on the bed thumbing through a big pile of elpees and fortyfives showing I am interested in who they all are and what they are singing, also some photographs. Big John is in the room saying hullo hullo hullo. Yes John how's tricks. Fine and that and you Sue. Hullo John. Back out he goes. The lassie's cousin big John. I never knew that. And her big sister Annie and brother-in-law Frank my old mate into the bargain and this wee sister is browned off as well I know with all the play of the front room and that with men and their wives and the back and forth repartee and the rest of it wishing she wasnt whatever age she is and married or engaged or even winching steady or. And she is leading me on not knowing what she is doing probably or maybe she does if she is at least eighteen or nineteen or seventeen or fifteen for fuck sake no but she cant be or big John would have spoken out which he might still do if I go ben fill up my glass. Good looking lassie Sue. Not bad yourself. Bit young but. Not so young as you think. Aye, easier to kiss through in the front room with all of them there like she says I did but here, and she's wondering what's up when the door opens and in comes Frank after a pause as Sue breaks off to play another record. O says the embarrassed big brother-in-law and mate Frank, I thought you were away home man. At the same time backing out the door to my smile and Sue's laugh as it clicks shut on us. Under orders from Annie maybe. I say to Sue they're probably thinking we're going to the naughty games ben here. Aye, a smile. Well. How's it going Sue. The married man I am shoves the hand up her skirt and upwards without thought forgetting I dont know her intimate at all between the thighs where her warmth begins and all she does is smile a bit Jesus Christ Sue and I am to take her now screw her I am supposed to with no lock on the door and everybody in the front room knowing what's what and Annie most likely egging on her man to come through throw me out etcetera Sue lying back and so making those thighs spread a little for me Christ Sue while she is humming with the song her skirt up fankled and wait I have to bar the door surely. I have to. I have to bar it. She waiting there look, not moved an inch nor said a word but the smile still with closed eyelids and me the pretend the chair will hold the door yet does it open in or out the way for Christ sake back by her side and the realisation but hot too hot and the shakes nervous hands and knees twitching I with effort make contact lips to lips touching no other part of her body I see rising to meet me but I dont but kiss deep and stroking her hair at the nape taking my weight on the left elbow from habit maybe or making up for the first direct thing I did too early on I think yet maybe it was fine if meant to be seducing though Jesus it must have been habit only, and now this kissing on its own even too much increasing the twitching me the randiness uncontrolled and the knowledge of in the front room and all me of before tomorrow and the wife and the rest of it the thought now gone Sue and not a movement and Christ sake if she moved I could do but no I am to act on my own the bad bastard I will be less sense or I can see any

Who's there, says Sue and sitting up placing her hand on my thigh. Me, calls her big sister Annie. We're just listening to the records, says Sue and moving her hand along where the warmth. Alright but will I bring the sandwiches through or what. Are you making them. Yes, what kind d'you want. What kind're you doing, and as speaking this last Sue's hand smoothing onto my balls outlining my hardon there between thumb and indexfinger. And cheese gammon. Gammon for me. What about. And Annie hesitating not saying my name. Gammon says Sue. Gammon's fine. Okay then from Annie. And are you making tea or coffee asks Sue slowly as she is unzipping the fly enjoying her sister and me when Annie answers the young sister has the hand inside the pants pulling out my cock and setting it alight all the time staring at the door question on question so her sister will stay there and I have to put my hand over hers for reasons, and Annie goes for supper. Stretching fully back on the bed Sue laughing to herself and not to me exactly as I realise it is she lying not doing and me in the know means I have difficulties in carrying on where I left off earlier which has to be the case I know. Hand to her breast which she likes but hard to say. Aye Sue I tell her, I know you. Nobody'll come in though. You cant know that for sure. But she says nothing. You cant know it for a certainty. She shrugs, it's okay. But I have lost it and considering a smoke and fresh drink right now she sits up and changes the record jumping the needle slightly, saying she likes this next one coming on and leaning her head on my arm at the shoulder her hand on my chest like the pictures and even tickles my ear so okay, okay, my fly is zipped now I spread her down on the bed again the way she was and. Just close your eyes Sue. I take her tights down so far and the same with the pants in a maybe professional slow way to get her going and that again though she maybe hasnt left off at all just me taking that for granted because it is so with me and the blouse out from the skirtband and unbuttoned just lifting the bra over her breasts and catching the nipple between teeth and tongue and my fingers inside her stroking down and down using my mouth when Annie comes back along with the food perhaps and knocks the door with young sister Sue arms downwards hands holding my head there and so nothing unable to move less I take myself from her and I have to do that Sue sitting up and chatting to big sister and now nude and getting the trousers down and playing with my hard thing all the time asking the questions and as Annie is answering this one she has moved her mouth forwards clinging along the tip with me there back lying out the game on the bed there and no not able to move at all knowing that door can open right now with Annie bursting straight in on wee sister Sue there doing me and me not moving but one muscle if the whole front room wife wean and in-laws all jump in together no I'll still be lying here out the game with Sue and me and her mouth and all of it Christ I'm finished Sue because of you and me.

Acid

In this factory in the north of England acid was essential. It was contained in large vats. Gangways were laid above them. Before these gangways were made completely safe a young man fell into a vat feet first. His screams of agony were heard all over the department. Except for one old fellow the large body of men was so horrified that for a time not one of them could move. In an instant this old fellow who was also the young man's father had clambered up and along the gangway carrying a big pole. Sorry Hughie, he said. And then ducked the young man below the surface. Obviously the old fellow had had to do this because only the head and shoulders — in fact, that which had been seen above the acid was all that remained of the young man.

The Melveille Twins, page 82

The long feud between the Melveille Twins was resolved by a duel in which stipulations of rather obvious significance had been laid down, the two men were bound back to back by a length of thick hemp knotted round their waists. Having gained choice of weapon the elder had already decided upon the cutlass and insofar as the younger is noted as having been 'corrie-fistit',[1] to infer a hint of possible irony may not be misguided. Few events of a more bloodthirsty nature are thought to have occasioned in the country of Scotland.

When the handkerchief fell the slashing began; within moments the lower part of each body was running red with blood. While wielding the weapon each held the empty hand aloft as though unwilling so much as to even touch the other. Eventually the small group of men silently observing, made their way off from the scene — a scene that for them had soon proved sour.

Only one man remained. He seems to have been a servant of some sort but little is known of his history aside from the fact of his being fairly literate.

The affair appeared at an end when the elder twin stumbled and together they landed on the ground. But almost immediately each had rolled in such a manner they were lying on the hands that grasped the weapons: for a brief period they kicked at each other. Coming to them with a jug of fresh water

1 To be 'corrie-fistit' in certain parts of Scotland, is to be left handed — even in the present day.

and strips of a clean material, the man bathed their wounds. He then lifted and placed the weapons outwith their arms' reach; he departed at this point. Whether the actual duel ended here is an open question. We are only certain that the feud ceased.

Zuzzed

A load of potatoes was stacked and waiting for me first thing that morning. I got right into it. The farmer's boy brought the jug of tea and once he had gone I sat down to roll a smoke. It was empty, the tin, just a bit of dust it contained. I jumped back at the work. Later he returned for the jug and though he would've seen I hadnt touched it he said nothing. I steamed into the weighing and packing, not stopping at all although when the lorry arrived in from the fields there was still plenty of the original left. The farmer helped the Frenchmen lug it in to me area while I continued. They finished. The farmer stood watching me work for a time. Yes, he said, we're getting a fair crop scotti.

I nodded as I carried across another tub of spuds to the weighing machine. I didnt notice him leave. I might have heard the lorry revving or something, gears maybe — the driver was hopeless.

Each tub or barrel of potatoes weighed out 28lbs so it wasnt too bad except if the farmer was about which meant it could only be 28lbs and nothing more or less. It was the constant bending fucked me. The shoulders get it, and the belly muscles. And the heat was terrific — the sweat I mean, I dont know how hot it was in the barn though outside maybe 70 to 80 degrees. I was working stripped to the waist. Clouds of dust all the time, streaks of sweat, the tidemarks everywhere. When dinner time came I wasnt hungry anyway. A bottle of cider would've went down fine right enough but apart from that nothing, nothing at all bar the smoke, of course, tobacco would've been ideal. Not so good being without it, there was just dust in the tin.

The Frenchmen were lugging in the next load. Only French worked the fields, some women with them and — when one of the men needed a slash for christ sake he just carried on never mind the women being there or not, a couple of girls amongst them but no, it never bothered them at all, just got on with it. Maybe that's healthy, who knows. Though the women never helped with the lugging off the lorry, they usually — christ knows, maybe off for a piss for god sake.

Warm out scotti! The farmer was there. I hadnt seen him. I was swinging a sack down from the pile and getting it across to the empty tubs in a movement. He stepped to the side just in time. Fair crop, he was saying.

I had dumped an empty next to the machine and was rolling in the spuds and while I topped it to the 28 mark I said; Can you loan me a nicker?

What was that scotti?

A nicker. Can you loan me a nicker? — a pound I mean, eh?

I knew he was looking at me but I continued with the work. A moment later he said, Yes, I told you about that, these Frenchmen, wily set of buggers, you have to watch it with these dominoes.

What — aye, yes, aye, can you loan me it then? take it off the wages and that.

He lit his pipe and exhaled, Dare say so scotti yes.

Fine.

Well then, he said. And while I was swinging across another sack he wound up by adding, Back to the field I suppose.

Moments later the lorry was revving. I couldnt believe it. By the time I ran out into the sun I saw it turning out onto the main drag, all the Frenchmen and women sitting on the back of it, laughing and joking quietly. A couple of them gave me a brief wave. I shook my head. A hen or a cock or something came walking across out of a fence thing. I looked at it. I went back into the barn. When the boy came with the afternoon jug I asked him if his old man had left anything for me. He stared at

me. A message son, I said, did your old man leave a message for
me?

No.

He was supposed to — a pound note it was. Maybe he left it
with your mother eh? Away and ask her.

He wont have.

Ask and see.

But he wont have.

Christ sake son will you go and do what I'm saying.

He came back in five minutes, shaking his head. He probably
had walked about the place and not bothered even seeing her.
He stood watching me for a bit then said, When're you taking
the tea scotti?

Eh . . . does she smoke son, your mother?

No.

Christ.

She wants to finish the washing up. The jug.

What. I stopped the weighing and turned and the fucking
barrel fell, the spuds all rolling about the fucking floor. The boy
stepped back out the road. It's okay son, it's okay, just take the
thing away.

The next load was the last for me although the French would
be picking until 8 p.m. Their morning began at 5 a.m. I
wouldnt've worked hours like that. The farmer had asked me a
couple of days back: Are you interested in a bit of overtime for
fuck sake! 5 till 8. Why in the name of christ did they do it! The
dough of course. By the time I had cleared and swept the area
and shot off home and got back the following morning another
load of fucking sacks would be stacked there ready and waiting.

The farmer was hovering around again. He went off and I
heard him calling over a couple of Frenchmen to give me a
hand with the travail. I got the time on one of their watches. I
stopped work. I looked at the farmer. Well scotti, he said,
taking the pipe out of his pocket. A good day's work eh? See
you in the morning then.

I couldnt believe my ears. I stared at him. He was patting the
tobacco down and when he noticed me he added, Alright?

My hands were trembling. I clasped them, rubbed them on the sweat rags I wore round my waist.

Something wrong then?

Something wrong! What d'you mean something wrong! My christ that's a fucking good yin right enough, a miserable bastarn nicker as well you'd think it was the crown fucking jewels or something.

He went tugging on the stem of his pipe. I grabbed my T-shirt and walked out the place. I heard him start and exclaim: The pound. Scotti! The pound. Sorry.

He was digging into his hip pocket for that big thick wallet and the Frenchmen standing smiling but curious as well. Forgot all about it, said the farmer, coming towards me while unwrapping a single.

Sorry. Sorry by christ, that is a good yin, a beauty. I continued on and out of the yard and kept on until about halfway between the farm and the turnoff, heading up towards the site where the tent was pitched. Then I stopped and sat at the side of the track. I sat on the turf, my feet on the caked mud in the ditch. I had forgotten to parcel a few spuds for my tea. Also the tin but it only had dust in it anyway. I had also forgotten a piece of string for my jeans. I was meaning to buy a belt, I kept forgetting and the threads at the cuffs of the jeans were dragging when I walked. The string would do meantime then I could get the belt. I got up, stiff at the knees. I strode along swinging my arms straight and on beyond the shortcut between hedges further on up to the front of the field where the tent was and left wheeling across the place, a few holiday-makers were wandering about with cooking utensils.

I was lying on top of the groundsheet, cool, the breathing coming short, in semi gasps maybe. I relaxed. Slowing down, slowing down, allowing the shoulders and the belly and the knees, letting them all get down, relaxing, the limbs and everything just slackly, calm, counting to ten and beyond, deep breathing exercises now, begin, and out in out in out in hold it there and the pulse rate lessens the heart pumps properly slowly does it slowly does it now yes and that fresh air is swirling down in these shadowy regions cleaning the lungs so now you can smoke and be okay and live to a ripe old age without having to halt every few yards to catch your breath, yes, simply continue and.

The sacks were piled high next morning. The lorry long gone to the fields. My mouth was sticky. I opened the tin and sniffed the dust. The boy had poked his head in and disappeared as soon as he saw me. Away to tell his mother probably. Fuck the pair of them. Later the crashing of gears and the lorry coming in. The Frenchmen with the load. I was getting a few looks. Fuck them as well. Then the farmer. Looking as unamazed as he could. Fuck you too. I laid down the barrel I was filling and went over. A nicker, I said, that's all I'm asking, till payday, just deduct it.

Of course scotti . . . He was taking out the pipe.

I mean just now, you know, it's just now I need it.

He nodded and got the wallet out, passed me a single.

Great. Fine. I nodded, I'm just going.

He looked at me.

The wee shop in the village just, I'll only be a minute . . . I grabbed the T-shirt.

By the grassy verge beneath the veranda of the local general store with the morning sun on my shoulders, the tin lying open at one side and the cider bottle uncorked on the other, and the cows lowing in the adjacent meadow, and the smoke rolled and being lighted and sucking in that first drag, keeping the thrapple shut to trap it there; with no bout of coughing, not a solitary splutter, the slight zuzz in the head. Instead of exhaling in the ordinary way I widened my lips and opened the throat without blowing so that the smoke just drifted right out and back in through my nostrils. Dizziness now but the head was clear though the belly not so good, and a shudder, fine. Then the cider, like wine it tasted and not too pleasant, just exact, and ready now, the second drag.

Time had passed. The lorry. It came into view, chugging along, the farmer at the wheel. I gestured at him with the bottle and the smoke, but as a greeting only. He returned it cheerily. The French on the back, the women there. I waved. Bon, I shouted. Once it had passed from view I swallowed the remainder of the cider and got up to return the bottle. I walked back to the farm, the tea would soon be coming.

A wide runner

I was in London without much cash and having to doss in the porch of a garden shed; it lay behind the shrubbery section of a grass square which the locals referred to as a park. The man who maintained it was called Kennedy. When he found me asleep he didnt kick me out but wanted to know what was what, and he left some sacking for me that evening. Next morning he brought John along with him; inside the shed he brewed a pot of tea. It was good and hot, burned its way down — late autumn or early winter. He got me answering the same questions for John's benefit; when I finished he looked to him. John shrugged, then muttered something about getting me a start portering if I wanted, interview that afternoon maybe. With a bit of luck I could even be starting the following morning.

Christ that's great, I said.

If he cant do it then nobody can, chuckled Kennedy. He's the blue-eyed boy in there!

John grimaced.

Yeh. Kennedy winked at me. Gets away with murder he do!

John shook his head, moments later he left.

At 8 a.m. next day I was kitted out with the uniform then being introduced to the rest of the squad in the porter's lodge. The place was a kind of college and the duties I performed were straightforward. For the first few days John guided me round; we pushed barrows full of stationery and stuff though in his position — Head Porter — he wasnt supposed to leave the vicinity of the marble entrance hall. He also fixed me up with a sub from the Finance Office, one week's lying time being obligatory. It was a surprise; I hadnt asked him to do it. That's great, I said, I'll buy you a pint when we finish.

He glanced at the clock in the lodge and shrugged, Just gone opening-time Jock, buy me it now if you like.

Kennedy was on a stool at the bar. I ordered pints for the three of us and he nudged me on the ribs. Yeh, didnt I tell you? blue-eyed boy he is!

Leave off, muttered John.

But Kennedy continued chuckling. You'll be moving to a new abode then?

Aye, thanks — letting me use the shed and that.

He laughed. Us sassenachs arent all bad then eh!

Silly fucker, grunted John.

After work they showed me to a rooming house they reckoned might be suitable. The landlady was asking a month's rent in advance but they had prepared me for it and eventually she did settle for the same sum spread over the following four weeks. It was an ideal place for the time being. The college was less than 10 minutes' walk away. Round the corner lived Kennedy and his family while John rented a room further down the road, in a house managed by a middle aged Irish couple who tended to make a fuss of him — things like laundry and making a point of getting him in for Sunday dinner every week. They were a nice couple but John got slightly irritated by it. Yeh, he said, you're into the position where you got to go; you're letting them down if you dont.

It turned out his wife had been killed in an accident several years ago. I didnt discover the exact details but it seems to have been an uncommon kind, and made the newspapers of the day. One night he was drunk he told me he could never have married again, that she had been the greatest thing in his life. To some extent this would explain why people reacted to him as they did. And Kennedy was also right, John did get away with a lot.

Inside the college an ex-R.A.F. man had overall charge of the hourly-paid workers; he treated those under him as though they were servicing the plane he was to pilot, but he shied clear of John. Our dinner hours were staggered between 11.45 a.m. and 2.45 p.m. Unless totally skint John spent the entire three hours in the pub. If the ex-R.A.F. man needed to contact him he made a discreet call to the lodge and sent one of the older porters with the message. Not surprisingly a few people resented this special treatment; yet nothing was ever said directly to John. He was in his early sixties, as thin as a pole, his skin colouring a mixture of greys and yellows. He could be a bit brusque, short tempered, frequently ignoring people who were speaking to him. I got on fine with him. Once he realised my interest in horse racing wasnt confined to the winning and losing of money we got on even better. Money was probably the main reason why he affected people; John had won and done vast sums of the stuff; and while I was hearing many stories from him I was also hearing quite a few about him — and not always to his credit. A fair amount of respect was accorded him but often it would be tinged by that mixture of scorn and vague annoyance which non punters and small punters can display whenever the exploits of heavy gamblers are discussed. Kennedy was an example of this. Although he genuinely liked John, and enjoyed recounting tales of his past wins, he would finish with a wink and a snort . . . Yeh Jock, then me and the Mrs had to feed him for the next bleeding month.

A couple of weeks into the job I was given additional duties in the college refectory. Being the last porter in I had no option in the matter, but it suited me anyway. In return for rinsing the pots and the pans I could eat as much free grub as I wanted. It meant I didnt have to worry about eating in the evening. Also I was escaping from the lodge. Portering can be an extremely boring job. Much of the time was spent in and around the lodge; when John was available it was fine but if not the only conversation to be had centred on job-gossip or last night's television. It was the kind of job people either stuck for a month or remained until retiral; most of them had been there for years, and even the arrival of some nice looking female didnt particularly interest them. One of the morning duties involved the distribution of mail; this entailed journeying in and out of all the different offices. It seemed the kind of thing the porters would be working on a rota-system but they werent bothered at all; anybody who felt like it could do the rounds. It was good. The college employed a great many temporary staff from the office agencies and it became something to look forward to.

The woman in charge of the kitchen and refectory was another to make a fuss over John. She nagged him about eating. She wrapped left-over food in tinfoil and sent it to the lodge in time for the pub shutting. At this stage of the day John's actions were erratic, absentminded; he would stick the packages in his uniform pocket and forget all about them. You could be sitting having a drink with him at 10 p.m. and out one would come, the tinfoil unwrapped and John continuing the conversation as he munched on a couple of rashers of bacon. One time in the lodge a porter went into silent hysterics at the window. The rest of us crept over to see what was what. Out in the marble entrance hall John with a piece of shepherd's pie in one hand and a clutch of mashed potato in the other; a visiting dignitary was inquiring directions and John was gesticulating various routes between bites. Too much brown ale was the chief cause but added to that was his preoccupation with the afternoon's racing results. John bet daily. And nightly where possible. He had a credit account with the bookie over the road. Either he used the phone in the lodge or sent me, if he couldnt be bothered walking across. I placed quite a few bets for him, but not too many on my own behalf. I wasnt very interested at the time — horse racing had come to a complete standstill. Not because of the weather, but some unknown virus had swept through stables up and down the country. In an effort to check it the authorities postponed racing indefinitely. John was betting on greyhounds, the virus being strictly equine.

In his day he had been a regular round many of the London tracks and whenever he was holding a few quid he still liked to have a go. But at the present everything he touched went wrong. It was the kind of spell anybody goes through. With John it was bad though; he seemed to be tapping dough from everywhere, from anybody; and the way things were about him it quickly became common knowledge. I got irritated when I heard them talking in the lodge or the pub but there was little to be said. By tapping their money he gave them the opportunity. Its unusual to meet anybody with the credit he had. He could be skint on a Wednesday morning but filling his place at the bar at dinner time, having a bet in the afternoon and meeting you in the pub late on in the evening. He had sources all over the place. Yet even so, gradually, he was returning from the pub before 2.45 p.m.; if making a bet he would do so only in cash and get me to carry it to another bookie; in the evening he would mutter an excuse and go home early. He was taking a real hammering.

The equine virus caused great deprivation. Before Xmas, as a special treat for starved horse punters like myself, an enterprising television team crossed the English Channel to screen back three races from a meeting in France. It was a Saturday and the British bookies were offering an almost complete race by race service. Both of us had worked overtime in the morning and in the pub afterwards I gave him another tenner, we went to the other betting shop. Although we knew next to nothing of the French form we did know the good jockeys and trainers and the rest of it. He laid the £10 on three crossed £2.50 doubles and a £2.50 treble. My own bet was more or less identical — I just selected different horses.

Back in the pub we watched his first two runners win. And then we watched his third runner win.

That third winner is the magical side of life. According to the betting forecast in the *'Life* the horse was a 7/2 chance. But the *pari mutuel* returned a dividend amounting to slightly more than 25/1.

Twenty five times your dough in other words.

When it flashed onto the television screen John paused then snorted; he glanced round at me, as if to say: These cunts think they're kidding me . . . And we rushed away to the betting shop for confirmation. It was true, and his winnings amounted to more than £1200. There wasnt enough on the premises to pay out in full but he was quite happy to wait until Monday morning. While the man behind the counter was getting the cash together John walked to study form at a greyhound meeting also taking place that afternoon. He backed the next favourite for £300. The man had to phone his head office to have it okayed. I was watching John. He was really shot through with nerves and yet I doubt whether a stranger could have noticed. At the best of times he got the shakes, but during the period in the betting shop he seemed to have been making a conscious effort to control himself. He stood with his hands in his trouser pockets, staring up at the results' board; usually his shoulders were round but now he was holding them as straight as he could. The greyhound favourite won at 7/4. When the result was announced he hesitated, he glanced at me then back to the board; finally he nodded. Yeh, he said, that'll do.

On the way back to his house we stopped off at the licenced grocer where he purchased a crate of brown ale, plus two bottles of gin which he passed onto the Irish couple. It was the only occasion I was ever in his room. There were a few knick-knacks and family photographs, and a big pile of old *Evening Standards* heaped in a corner. A fusty smell hung about the place. He noticed my reaction. Fucking pong, he said, open a window if you like. Then taking two cups from a cupboard he passed me one along with a bottle of brown ale, and he continued talking. He was defending greyhounds. It wasnt that I didnt like them, just that it was almost impossible getting a line to their form without actually visiting the track to see them race. He admitted this but went on to tell me about an old mate he used to have. He had told me about him before, in connection to a system he worked. In fact, according to John, his old mate worked it so successfully that the bookies refused to deal with it across their betting shop counter. The guy was forced into going to the track to make his bets with the on-course fraternity.

The system is quite well known, nothing startling; it's called the stop-at-a-winner and in principle consists of a minimum 1 bet with a maximum of 4. You select your four dogs and back the first to win; if it loses you back the second; if it loses you back the third; if it loses you back the fourth; if it loses you've done the money. The cash outlay on the first doubles onto the second and triples onto the third, quadruples onto the fourth; if your initial stake was £10 and you choose four losers then you wind up doing £100 i.e. bets of £10, £20, £30 and £40.

The beauty of the system lies in this stopping-at-a-winner; as soon as a dog wins the bet stops automatically. Only one solitary winner from four is required and a profit is almost guaranteed. In theory to choose one winner from four is not too difficult. It is not certain and by no means easy, but still and all, it should not be too difficult — and one thing is certain, if the bookies dont like the bet then it cant be bad.

This is all fair enough, but like anything else it applies only under normal circumstances. When somebody's on a losing streak everything can go crazy. Odds-on shots run like 100/1 chances; all these stonewall racing certainties that should win in a canter, they all fall at the last fucking fence. The one thing they all have in common is that you've backed them. It reaches the stage where you feel guilty about choosing a favourite because of the disservice you're doing to all the rest of the punters. I was reminding John about that kind of stuff. He smiled briefly, then he sniffed and got up off his chair; he walked to the corner of the room and lifted a bunch of the old newspapers; he produced a quantity of various coloured pens. Jock, he said, I been wanting to have a go at this for years. While he was speaking he sorted through the back editions, opening out their respective dog-sections, spreading them along the floor. You got to play it wide, he said, that's all; you just got to play it wide. What you do Jock, you cut out the fucking middle man. Yeh, he said, the fucking middle man — you know who that is? its you, you and me, we're the fucking middle man. Yeh, he said, open another couple of bottles.

He halved the quantity of pens. That old guy he was telling me about had eventually gone skint for different reasons but the most important was his method of selection; he didnt really have one, he just chose the dogs from his own reading of the formbook. What you had to find was a genuine method, so that the four dogs would be chosen for you. And then there was

another thing to consider, which races to work it on. It would
be pointless using a system that forced you into hanging about
the track all night with money in the pocket. At most
greyhound meetings there are between 8 and 12 races. Probably
the best way out of the bother is to work it on the first four races
of the night; in that way you get in and get out — you arrive for
the first race and make your bet, and leave as soon as you back
the winner. And if you dont back a winner then you leave after
the fourth race, and maybe try again the next night.

Yeh, said John, you got to screw the nut.

Plenty of selection methods were available. For the following
couple of hours we set about testing as many as we could think
of, using the old back editions, working on the past meetings at
all the London tracks. Some useful information resulted. Many
dog punters use methods and one of the most common — next
to acting on the advice of racing journalists — is to bet on
particular trap numbers. In every race there are six dogs and
each goes from an individual trap numbered from 1 to 6. Over
the period we tested Trap 6 was by far the most successful; on
one occasion this draw had provided the winner of seven
consecutive races. But for the stop-at-a-winner system that
kind of consistency is irrelevant. All it required is one winner
out of four.

It was me who came up with the right one. The *time dog*. We
were both a bit surprised, and I was also a bit disappointed. The
time dog is the greyhound to have recorded the fastest time of
the six runners in their most recent races. To the non punter it
may seem obvious to say that the dog who runs the fastest will
race more quickly. Well it does seem obvious but it never works
out that way as most punters know. Too many variables exist
and, like everything else in the formbook, recent times are only
a guide.

But the fact remains that many punters who reckon
themselves expert on the subject will set more store on time
than any other factor. And this is why I was disappointed,
because our test seemed to prove them right. And if they were
right then how come they were usually so fucking skint. John

just shrugged. Well yeh, he said, but like I say Jock, most of them the cunts, they're looking to back 8 winners out of 8 fucking races.

Aye I know but still and all.

Open a couple of bottles.

Aye but John . . .

Look Jock, listen to me now; see I been watching this for years and I know what I'm fucking talking about. You got some important things here. Now what you got? you got a system, you got the stop-at-a-winner, right?

Aye.

So you know what you're doing for a fucking kick off. Most of them the cunts, they dont even know that, they dont know what the fuck they're doing! right? Now what else you get? yeh, the fucking dogs, you got them chose for you, you got them selected, right?

Aye but . . .

Right?

Right, aye.

Okay, so what else you got?

The *time dog*.

Yeh yeh, the *time dog*, that's how you got them chose — but what else you got?

Eh.

Come on Jock! He grinned and reached for the bottle I'd passed to him; he began pouring the brown ale into his cup. Then he sniffed, What else you got?

Well you need a lot of fucking luck.

No you dont! leave off! you dont need no fucking luck — why you think we got the fucking system! Jock, you got to play this wide.

Aye.

Now you take me, I'm a cunt. I'm a cunt Jock, no two ways about it. You go down the pub and ask any of them and they'll tell you, I'm a cunt.

I snorted.

And you, he said, you're a cunt. We're both cunts — you

know that — so what we got to do, we got to cut out the fucking middle man, right?

I shrugged.

Right?

Aye, right.

Okay . . . John took a mouthful of the beer, refilled the cup. What we do Jock, we work it together. Now we both know the score, we got to make the same bet and we got to take the same dogs. I mean Jock . . . he shrugged, look at this afternoon? Yeh, now I'm not criticizing, in your place I'd do the fucking same. But I lift a grand and you go skint. Yeh. John grinned suddenly. Fucking froggies, always did've a soft spot for the cunts.

First thing on Monday morning he disappeared from the college to open a bank account. The day before he spent out of the district, visiting his family but also repaying a few debts I think. He was allowing £400 for the system, that is, £200 apiece. Our initial bet was to be £10 so we needed £100 each for the stake; the extra £100 was for emergencies. I kept mine planked in my room; whether John did this or not I was never sure.

That first Monday went well although we saw little of each other till the late afternoon when we resumed chatting. Previous to this it seemed as if we werent chatting by some unspoken agreement, that it could have brought some bad luck on the system to continue discussing it all the time. He survived the day without a solitary bet. Even during his midday break he made a point of drinking less than he would normally have done. His dayshift started earlier than mine and so he clocked-off before me; we met in the pub for 7 p.m.; I just had time to swallow a pint and then the taxi was there and we were off.

An hour later we returned. The first runner had won a short head at 9/4, throwing us a profit of £22.50 apiece, less expenses. Next night to another track where the first two runners got beat but the third won a length at 7/2, giving us a profit of £75 each overall — almost twice the wage I was receiving weekly as a porter. It was very nice. And the obvious problem arose: how to continue going to work every day with all that cash in the pocket. Not that it bothered John. Put it this way, he said, at my fucking age what else I got to do.

During the next couple of weeks the *time dog* missed on two separate occasions; then came a losing sequence of three consecutive evenings. It was a bit of a bombshell. There's a funny sense in which you expect one to be followed by two. Since it had failed on individual evenings the worst I expected was that it would fail twice in a row. We went along for that third evening and I doubt whether I truly thought about what would happen if it failed again. As it turns out we had enough in hand to attend for the fourth night and the *time dog* won the second race at 6/1; and gradually we recouped the losses without having touched the emergency fund. We werent winning a fortune but it was paying.

When the equine virus vanished — as mysteriously as it had struck — it came as an anticlimax; horse racing remained at a standstill, the ground either waterlogged or bonehard. But the dogs went on chasing the parcel of fur. Some of these nights were freezing cold and making the trek across London could be a slog, particularly knowing you might be on the return journey half an hour later. There was one night John had to go a message on behalf of his family and we arranged to meet in the track bar. If he came late I was to double up on the bet to keep his side going. Wimbledon it was, and I made the journey by rail. But I wound up getting the two stations mixed up. The one I got off at was right in the middle of nowhere and I had to walk for miles, not a taxi in sight, and I missed the first three races. But John had arrived in time and he doubled up for me. To be honest, I could have done with a night off now and again; but I didnt broach the subject in case I hurt his feelings. Weekends were the worst — Fridays and Saturdays had come to resemble Tuesdays and Wednesdays. A lot can go on in London and it doesnt all take place at the track. A new shorthand typist had started in one of the college offices; when I brought in the mail we had reached the stage of avoiding each other's eyes. If I asked the girl out it had to be a Sunday, if not explanations were called for. I suppose I could have arranged to meet her after racing some evening but explanations would still have been called for. The routine we were into meant leaving the track together and taking a cab, or the tube if convenient, back to the local pub; once I had swallowed a couple of pints in there I could rarely be bothered moving.

John seemed to be enjoying the life. Almost every night somebody was coming across to ask how he was doing and where he had been hiding; frequently the company was good as well, and it might have been nice hanging on for the chat, but we couldnt, the essence of the system's success was this stopping-at-a-winner. We had to leave the track immediately; anything else would have been a risk. Systems have to be regular otherwise they arent systems. Oddly enough that side of things gave us a bit of status — in fact it isnt odd at all. In any racetrack in the country there is nobody more respected than the punter who comes to back one dog and one dog only. And whether it wins or not is fundamentally irrelevant. We told nobody about the system but those punters known to John must have become aware something was going on — as soon as we cheered home a winner we vanished.

At college and in the pub we said nothing either. A little minor hostility occurred early on, towards me. The pub regulars were seeing us go to the track and return from the track and because it was all being accomplished within an hour or so they assumed we were continually doing the money. Kennedy had acted a bit coldly, as if I was responsible for John's welfare, or maybe he reckoned I was just tagging along for poncing purposes. It was pointless explaining anything. It was still pointless when they realized we were backing winners. Occasionally a kind of daft undertone could be sensed, as though we were wasting time and money i.e. why fork out good cash on taxi fares and entrance fee when you dont even stay to watch the whole night's racing. It's difficult to say exactly. One of the daftest statements I ever heard came from Kennedy on that Saturday when John turned the £10 into £1200. It was unusual to find him in the pub at all. Saturday was the night he normally went out with his wife; if they came to the local they always sat through in the lounge. But that evening he was on his stool at the bar when we entered. John was playing it very cool, knowing everybody in the district would've heard the news — the rest of the regulars were doing their best not to let him see he had been the main topic of conversation since opening time. I got the pints in for the three of us. Kennedy didnt speak for quite a while, but he kept on grinning and shaking his head, now and then nudging me on the ribs. At last he winked and chuckled, Yeh Jock, we all got to start backing them French horses . . . Yeh, he said, we got to start backing them French horses . . . He laughed at John and swivelled on the stool. Hey lads! he called, we all got to start backing them French horses now!

The laughter was loud. John reacted by raising his eyebrows and studying the gantry. The guvnor came through from the lounge to see what was what and he grinned, and after a moment he said: Alright John?

John continued to study the gantry. When the laughter subsided he muttered, Silly fucker, but it went no further than that. I think he felt sorry for Kennedy. The man had a lot of good points but he had that bad habit of playing to the gallery, no matter at whose expense — his nights were rarely complete unless John unwrapped one of his tinfoil packages. Yet John was friendlier to him than he was to anybody else in the place. I saw him do something in the lodge once which would have crushed Kennedy. He had asked one of the porters for a match and the porter cracked a joke while passing him a boxful. This porter was known to be tight with his cash but still and all, I was there when it happened, and there didnt seem any genuine malice in the remark — it had something to do with people who gamble large sums of money but neglect to spend on the petty essentials. John turned and stared at the man for several moments; then he placed the box of matches on the table unused; and he started talking to another man as though the one in question was out of the room somewhere. The atmosphere was terrible. Nobody was able to look at the guy; and eventually he left the lodge without speaking.

I doubt if Kennedy could have recovered from something like that.

John left himself open to comment because he borrowed dough so indiscriminately. It was a thing about him I couldnt understand. During the bad time when he was losing he must have tapped every regular in the place, the same thing in the college — not just the lodge but the refectory, the kitchen and probably the offices as well. Once I knew him better I dug him up about it in the pub. Yeh, you're right, he said.

The second time the method failed three nights on the trot it coincided with a general thaw, and horse racing resumed on a fairly regular basis. Unlike the other time we now had to go into the emergency fund, but again we fought back to recoup the losses. It took a while but at least we were doing it, and we were still in the game. I was happy to ignore the horses; because of the long interruption the formbook would've been as well chipped out the window. It was a bookie's paradise, impossible to pick a winner. When a favourite actually did get first past the post you were expecting to see it headlined in the following morning's *'Life*. We were discussing this across at the track in company with a few people of John's acquaintance. For the past two nights snow had been falling thickly then melting during the day. The going was officially heavy but according to the experts this was a bit of an understatement, it was like a bog — particularly on the inside. The inside of the track receives more of a pounding than the outside; and on really heavy going the dogs who favour this side often race at a disadvantage, as though they're trying to run through porridge. In an effort to justify this the track authorities had strewn straw round the inside. But the early results were bad, and according to the punters in the bar, it was the straw to blame; contrary to expectations the dogs drawn on the inside were not simply holding their own, they were getting what amounted to a yard and a half of a start. The first three favourites all got beat without ever having been in the hunt. The same thing applied to the first three *time dogs*, two of whom had actually been the favourites. It was pathetic. Normally we at least got a cheer, but tonight we had hardly been able to raise a shout.

Down in the bar the conversation went on, with John taking his part, listening and occasionally nodding, rarely talking. As the merits of each greyhound was discussed for the fourth race I could hear the *time dog* being rejected mainly on the basis of its draw, it was to run from Trap 6. This dog was also an uncertain trapper — which means it sometimes started fast and other times started slow. Also, it liked to run its race on the wide outside of the track and so did the dog next to it, the one drawn in Trap 5. Also, this Trap 5 was known as a speedy trapper and thus more or less guaranteed to steal the ground from Trap 6. So what with this, that and the next thing Trap 6 wasnt reckoned much of a bet.

The warning bell sounded for the end of the dogs' parade and the company dispersed to lay out the money. John muttered, What d'you reckon Jock?

I had been half expecting it. How d'you mean? I said.

Them big wide runners, they're doing fuck all tonight. What d'you reckon? he sniffed. Reckon we should leave it out?

What?

He shrugged. And when I didnt reply he added, No use fucking throwing it away.

Ach! I shook my head and we left the bar, hurrying along to the betting-ring. They were making Trap 6 an 8/1 chance and as we stood there they moved it out to 10/1. See what I mean? he said, a no-hoper Jock — save the dough.

You must be joking.

He pursed his lips and paused, then made to say something but I shook my head and stepped over to the nearest bookmaker, and took the 10/1 for the £40. I held up the ticket for him to see. He indicated a bookie a few pitches along the rank who was making Trap 6 a 12/1 chance. He shook his head at me. I shrugged and left the betting-ring, went up to our place in the Stand. Shortly before the *off* he was there beside me, and that instant prior to the traps opening he told me he had backed the favourite.

Trap 2 was the favourite. The punters had gambled it off the board; from an opening show of 6/4 the weight of money going onto the thing had reduced its odds to 1/2. John didnt tell me how much he had stuck on the dog but at that kind of price he must have done it for plenty. According to the conversation in the bar the dog was a certainty to lead at the 1st bend and get the best of the going up the back straight; and by the time it hit the last bend the race would be all over bar the shouting. There was no shouting. Trap 6 shot out and led from start to finish — the kind of race when you can hear the dogs puffing and panting, because of the silence, the crowd totally stunned by what they're having to witness. I was also watching in silence. I collected my winnings and met him in the bar.

He had a drink ready for me but was apparently too engrossed in his racecard to make any comment. It was the first time we had ever been there beyond this fourth race. I began footering about with my own racecard, marking in comments on the running of the previous race — this was something I often did to pass the time.

John was watching me.

What's up? I said. I smiled.

He shook his head.

Ah well John, you've got to mark in the form and that.

Mark in the form . . . he said; you cunt! mark in the form!

Ach come on for fuck sake, I've backed a winner and you've backed a loser, it's as simple as that.

As simple as that! As simple as that . . . You cunt! He left his drink on the bar and strode out of the place. I stayed where I was. Before the start of the fifth race I walked up to the Stand and stood where we usually stood but he wasnt there and he didnt arrive back in the bar afterwards. Outside the track I had a quick look in a couple of the local pubs but he wasnt in any of them. I took a taxi up West.

I didnt bother going into the college on Monday or Tuesday, and I stayed away from the pub. On Wednesday we kept out of each other's road but from the way the manageress of the refectory gave me the tinfoil package for him I knew he had kept the thing secret. Towards clocking-out time he came looking for me while I was out pushing a stationery barrow. He apologised immediately. What a cunt, he said, always have been. You ask anybody Jock, they'll tell you.

I shrugged. It was just one of these things.

Several days later I was handing the uniform back into the ex-R.A.F. man and saying cheerio in the lodge. Even without the incident I would still have been leaving. It was a good few quid I had gathered, and the weather progressed, a nice hint of spring in the air. John was back hitting the betting shop every afternoon; as far as I heard he was taking a hammering. It was totally daft, the results were still far too erratic. And leaving that aside, there was only about a month to go before the start of the *flat season*. John was like me in that respect, things like the *jumping season* and greyhound racing only helped fill the winter break.

Ascot was his favourite course — for the Royal Meeting. Without fail he took his holidays in June each year. Well you got to go, he said, them's the best racehorses in the world.

He was superstitious about it. On numerous occasions he had been skint and June rapidly approaching. Then at the last possible moment he would get a turn, and everything would be fine. Yeh, he said, you believe it you dont believe it, it's all the same to me — but I've seen me, in it right up to the fucking eyeballs — cant show my face or the cunts, they'll be taking swipes at it, yeh — then bingo! right out the fucking blue — and I'm down there. Go on Lester! Go on my son!

That punters' dream again, the summer sunshine with strawberries and champagne, and Lester going through the card.

No longer the warehouseman

What matters is that I can no longer take gainful employment. That she understands does not mean I am acting correctly. After all, one's family must eat and wear clothes, be kept warm in the winter, and they must also view television if they wish — like any other family. To enable all of this to come to pass I must earn money. Thirteen months have elapsed. This morning I had to begin a job of work in a warehouse as a warehouseman. My year on the labour exchange is up — was up. I am unsure at the moment. No more money was forthcoming unless I had applied for national assistance which I can do but dislike doing for various reasons.

I am worried. A worried father. I have two children, a wife, a stiff rent, the normal debts. To live I should be working but I cannot. This morning I began a new job. As a warehouseman. My wife will be sorry to hear I am no longer gainfully employed in the warehouse. My children are of tender years and will therefore be glad to see me once more about the house although I have only been gone since breakfast time and it is barely five o'clock in the afternoon so they will have scarcely have missed me. But my wife: this is a grave problem. One's wife is most understanding. This throws the responsibility on one's own shoulders however. When I mention the fact of my no longer being the warehouseman she will be sympathetic. There is nothing to justify to her. She will also take for granted that the little ones shall be provided for. Yet how do I accomplish this without the gainful employment. I do not know. I dislike applying to the social security office. On occasion one has in the past lost one's temper and deposited one's children on the counter and been obliged to shamefacedly return five minutes later in order to uplift them or accompany the officer to the station. I do not like the social security. Also, one has difficulty in living on the money they provide.

And I must I must. Or else find a new job of work. But after this morning one feels one . . . well, one feels there is something wrong with one.

I wore a clean shirt this morning lest it was expected. Normally I dislike wearing shirts unless I am going to a dinner dance etcetera with the wife. No one was wearing a shirt but myself and the foreman. I did not mind. But I took off my tie immediately and unbuttoned the top two buttons. They gave me a fawn dusk or dust perhaps coat, to put on — without pockets. I said to the foreman it seemed ridiculous to wear an overcoat without pockets. And also I smoke so require a place to keep cigarettes and the box of matches. My trouser pockets are useless. My waist is now larger than when these particular trousers were acquired. Anything bulky in their pockets will cause a certain discomfort.

One feels as though one is going daft. I should have gone straight to the social security in order to get money. Firstly I must sign on at the labour exchange and get a new card and then go to the social security office. I shall take my B1 and my rent book and stuff, and stay calm at all times. They shall make an appointment for me and I shall be there on time otherwise they will not see me. My nerves get frayed. My wife knows little about this. I tell her next to nothing but at other times tell her everything.

I do not feel like telling my wife I am no longer the warehouseman and that next Friday I shall not receive the sum of twenty five pounds we had been expecting. A small wage. I told the foreman the wage was particularly small. Possibly his eyes clouded. I was of course cool, polite. This is barely a living wage I told him. Wage. An odd word. But I admit to having been aware of all this when I left the labour exchange in order that I might commence employment there. Nobody diddled me. My mind was simply blank. My year was up. One year and six weeks. I could have stayed unemployed and been relatively content. But for the social security. I did not wish to risk losing my temper. Now I shall just have to control myself. Maybe send the wife instead. This might be the practical solution. And the clerks shall look more favourably upon one's wife. Perhaps increase one's rate of payment.

I found the job on my own. Through the evening times sits vac col. It was a queer experience using the timecard once more. Ding ding as it stamps the time. I was given a knife along with the overcoat. For snipping string.

I am at a loss. At my age and considering my parental responsibilities, for example the wife and two weans, I should be paid more than twenty five pounds. I told the foreman this. It is a start he replied. Start fuck all I answered. It is the future which worries me. How on earth do I pay the monthly rent of £34.30. My wife will be thinking to herself I should have kept the job till securing another. It would have been sensible. Yes. It would have been sensible. Right enough. I cannot recall the how of my acceptance of the job in the first instance. I actually wrote a letter in order to secure an interview. At the interview I was of course cool, polite. Explained that my wife had been ill this past thirteen months. I was most interested in the additional news, that of occasional promotional opportunities. Plus yearly increments and cost of living naturally. Word for word. One is out of touch on the labour exchange. I knew nothing of cost of living allowance. Without which I would have been earning twenty two sixty or thereabouts.

It is my fault. My wife is to be forgiven if she . . . what. She will not do anything.

There were five other warehousemen plus three ware-houselads, a forklift driver, the foreman and myself. At teabreak we sat between racks. An older chap sat on the floor to stretch his legs. Surely there are chairs I said to the foreman. He looked at me in answer. Once a man had downed his tea I was handed the empty cup which had astonishing chips out of its rim. It was kind of him but I did not enjoy the refreshment. And I do not take sugar. But the tea cost nothing. When I receive my first wage I am to begin paying twenty five pence weekly. I should not have to pay for sugar. It does not matter now.

Time passes. My children age. My wife is in many ways younger than me. She will not say a word about all this. One is in deep trouble. One's bank account lacks money enough. I received a sum for this morning's work but it will shortly be spent. Tomorrow it is necessary I return to the labour exchange. No one will realise I have been gone. Next week should be better. If this day could be wiped from my life or at least go unrecorded I would be happy.

The warehousemen were discussing last night's television. I said good god. A funny smell. A bit musty. Soggy cardboard perhaps.

The boss, the boss — not the foreman — is called Mr Jackson. The foreman is called George. The boss, he . . . The trouble is I can no longer. Even while climbing the subway stairs; as I left the house; was eating my breakfast; rising from my bed; watching the television late last night: I expected it would prove difficult.

Mr Jackson, he is the boss. He also wears a shirt and tie. Eventually the express carriers had arrived and all of we warehousemen and warehouselads were to heave to and load up. It is imperative we do so before lunch said Mr Jackson. I have to leave I said to him. Well hurry back replied George. No, I mean I can no longer stay I explained. I am going home. And could I have my insurance cards and money for this morning's work. What cried Mr Jackson. George was blushing in front of Mr Jackson. Could I have my cards and money. It is imperative I go for a pint and home to see the wife.

I was soon paid off although unable to uplift my insurance cards there and then.

The problem is of course the future — financing the rearing of one's offspring etcetera.

Keep moving and
no questions

It was my own fault. My planning never seems to allow of action of an intentional nature. I can always bring myself right to a point where some sort of precipice appears odds on to be round a corner. But this bringing-of-myself appears to be an end in itself; nothing further happens which can squarely be laid as an effect of my own volitions. Terrible state of affairs. I had arrived back in London fine, as conceived, was ambling around the Kings Cross Area quite enjoying seeing the old places. Next thing a publican was calling Time Gentlemen Please and I was stranded. Nowhere to go. Nothing fixed. Never anything fixed. This fixing business . . . I dont know about this fixing business at all. Obviously getting here was sufficient otherwise something further would have been transpiring. And something further could easily have been a straightforward sign-in at a cheap bed & breakfast of which the Kings Cross Area has more than a few. The money right enough. The money could have been one subliminal motive for my lack of the leap forwards. I wasnt too well fixed. Fixed. Not fixed again.

I was watching this drop of water on the tip of an old woman's nose. It didnt quiver. We were sitting on a bench at a busstop outside St Pancras Station. The rain had stopped some twenty minutes ago. I got a bar of chocolate from a machine. Fifteen pence it cost me. The old yin took the piece I offered and chewed on it for a long time. She had no teeth and was probably allowing this chocolate to slide back and forth over her gums, wearing it down while increasing the saliva flow. She never spoke. Stared straight ahead. I was to her right. I doubt whether she knew I was watching her; doubt whether it would have bothered her anyway. She didnt smoke and I found this surprising. I lighted my own. Although she moved slightly her gaze never altered. The drop of water had gone from her nose. Then the rain again, a slow drizzle. I rose from the bench, making more noise than necessary when I lifted my bag; for some reason I reckoned a quiet movement might have disturbed her.

Along towards Euston I walked. Night lights glinting on the pavement, on the roads and on the roofs and glass fronts of office buildings. And on the moon as well; a moon in full view, to be beheld during this drizzle. I was no longer ambling now. And a good thing this; it was somehow sending me on ahead of myself. Yet at the same time I was aware of the possibility of missing out on something a more leisurely stroll could perhaps have allowed me to participate within. On up, Tavistock way. Nobody about. A brisk pace. My boots were fairly able; no misgivings about stepping into puddles. Across and towards the British Museum and around the back in the shadows, and around the front and back around the back and back around the whole thing again for Christ sake.

Onwards. Figures appearing hailing taxi-cabs, going home to their places out the rain. More lighting now, brighter on the main road. Through into the rear of Soho where my pace lessened. Smaller buildings, narrower pavements, railings and basements; rain drops plopping off the edges of things; occasionally sharp lighting giving out from windows where folk would be gathered, snugly. One basement in particular with its iron gate at the top lying ajar. Downstairs I went slowly. A sign on the wall: two quid to enter. Music. One please, I said to this guy inside the lobby who gave out no ticket and stuffed the money into this pocket on the breast of his shirt, buttoning the flap down on it.

The push door made a creaking sound. The lighting dim. A girl singing in this English voice. An English traditional song she was singing in this icy voice. An odd voice; not a voice without feeling. A direct voice, and reminiscent of a singer whose name I couldnt quite rake out although I used to hear her fairly often at one time. All the people there; a lot sitting down on the floor with their backs to the wall, others lying with their hands clasped behind their heads or sitting cross-legged. Couples with arms about shoulders and heads on shoulders. All listening to the girl singing her song.

I sat down in a space next to the back wall and after a moment closed my eyelids. When I opened them again the space to my right had increased to around five yards and a girl was kneeling on the floor with her arms folded. She was alone — but in this direct fashion. Her head stiffly positioned, the neck exactly angled. Only her shoulders twitched. The position must have been uncomfortable. The small of her back there — I can make the curved motion with my hand. And yet only her shoulders made any movement whatsoever!

I closed my eyelids. Footsteps. It was a man making towards her, his manner of moving was only to her though he walked loosely as he threaded the way between people. And now the girl's shoulders were not even twitching. She had edged her feet from her shoes. Her toes seemed to be maintaining a sort of plumb point — and her arms! — folded in this direct fashion. Jesus.

He paused a fraction when he arrived, then dropped to his knees, his hands placed on the floor to balance, fingertips pointing on to the side of her limbs he was facing her. But she continued to stare at the singer. Poised there, only her toes working.

He could kneel by her all night but it would still be finished. I could have told him that. She half turned her shoulder and said about three words; her eyes had remained in the direction of the singer. Then the shoulders returned to their former position. His time was up. Your time's up I said without opening my mouth.

He left, but he was not making a retreat. He was just making his way away from her. Eventually the girl swivelled her knees to stretch out her legs, moved to rest her back against the wall. She opened her handbag but after a brief glance inside she closed it over. She placed it to the blind side from me. I could see her toes now exercising, her knees, and her neck; until finally she relaxed. A bit later I rose to see if they served coffee; I left my chattels lying on the spot.

I bought two and back inside I handed one across to her. Put it to the side of her. Look, I said, all I'm doing is giving you this coffee. Nothing else. Just a coffee. Just take a drop of this coffee.

She didnt reply.

I'm leaving it lying there, I said. You should drink it. I'm not doing anything. Just giving you this coffee to drink.

She lifted it. The eyes passed over me. She took a little sip at it. Jesus Christ; well well well.

Pardon, she said.

I didnt answer. I lighted a cigarette and inhaled deeply. Too much for me. Everything. The way she could do it all. Even the man. He could do it all as well. Jesus. It was bad. I had the arrival for a plan. An arrival! Dear God. Hopeless. It was bad. Pardon?

What . . . I glanced at her. I must have spoken aloud. Maybe the bad or the hopeless.

Nothing . . . I said. I was only . . . Couldnt even finish the sentence. With a slight nod she looked away from me. I closed my eyelids. But they opened immediately. Look, I said, will you take a smoke? I saw you footering around in your handbag and I was going to offer then but decided against it — not a real decision — not something I . . . A cigarette. Will you take a cigarette from me?

She nodded. I passed her one.

My coffee was lukewarm. It had never really been hot either. I shuddered on draining the last third of it. I dont mind lukewarm tea but never seem to have got the taste for lukewarm coffee. The singer had stopped for a breather and her band were playing a medley of some kind. Some of the audience had risen and were moving around on the floor.

I glanced at the girl. She was smoking in a serious way although she let out big mouthfuls of smoke before inhaling; and when she exhaled this last stuff she did so making an O shape of her mouth so that the smoke came out in firm columns. Food. A meal, I said, fancy a meal. Nothing startling. Just a plate of chips or something in a snackbar. Nothing else involved. I just feel like a plate of chips and taking you for one as well, eh? Fancy it. That coffee was murder polis.

Pardon?

That coffee. Terrible. Lukewarm to begin with I think. No chance of enjoyment from the start. Fancy a plate of chips? Scotch?

Aye, yes. what d'you say? — you coming?

She hesitated, another cloud of smoke before the inhaled lot emerging in its fixed shape. She said, To be honest I . . .

Nothing else involved. I'm not doing anything. Look, I said, all I want to do is get a plate of chips and take you for one as well. Too much for me. All of it.

What?

Ach. Fuck it. What a carry on. I dont know . . . can never really get it all connecting in an exact manner. Out it all seems to come. She was not bothering though. Knew what I was saying, she knew it fine well. I was just . . . passes the time: I said. Keeps you warm — plate of steaming chips and a piping hot cup of fresh tea.

You'll have to wait till I collect my things, she answered; I'll meet you at the door.

The guy with my two quid in his breast pocket was standing pretending not to have noticed me there hanging about with my bag. She came along carrying an enormous suitcase. Jesus, must be emigrating or something.

Pardon?

Your suitcase — looks like it contains the life possessions.

O. I was staying with friends over the week. Just got back this evening. She pointed at my effort.

I nodded: Deceiving bag this. Takes everything, all of the chattels. Good buy. Got it in a sale a couple of years back. Strong stuff it's made out of.

I held the door open and we went upstairs. The rain still drizzling down. I could not think of where to go for allnight snackbars. There is one, she said, not too far.

Suitcase — it looks heavy. I'll take a hold of it for you, eh?

No, I can manage.

What a surprise.

Pardon?

Nothing . . . I was just . . . I'm starving. While since I ate anything.

While she was walking she looked straight ahead, and always somehow half a pace in front or behind me. Buildings and basements and the rest of it: none of this interested her whatsoever. On she went. A place near Charlotte Street. I ordered the grub. No words spoken during the eating. I made to get another two cups of tea but she said: No — not for me.

There were other people in the snackbar, many were chatting and she must have been aware of this in relation to herself and the situation because she began glancing at the door.

Well, I said.

I better be going home.

I know that. Nothing else of course. I wasnt worrying about that.

We're not supposed to be out late, she said.

Late by Christ it must be near — Ach, doesnt matter.

Outside the snackbar she was set to go off alone. Half turning to me she said: Thanks.

No bother. Hang on and I'll get you home. And dont worry. I'm not . . .

Honestly, she said, I'll make it all right on my own. I dont live far from here. Bye.

Too much for me. Absolute nonsense. Far too much. Plate of chips and a cup of tea I mean that was precisely the case and nothing else involved. Same as the walking home, passes the time. I'm not, Jesus, ach.

But I'm only round the corner, she said.

Fuck all to do with me where you are. I'm not doing anything. Just hanging about till it all begins this morning. Still dark as well, you're best taking no chances — never know who's around.

She shrugged: Alright then, thanks.

Back along in the direction of the British Museum till she halted outside of a place, the place where she lived. It's run by nuns, she said. I must go in.

Aye.

At the top of the short flight of stairs she half turned but without actually seeing me. She said: Bye.

Aye.

When she closed the door after her the light went on in the hall. I hung about waiting for a time. Nothing whatsoever happened. The light went out. But no other light came on upstairs. Maybe she lived at the back of the building or in the basement. More than quarter of an hour I stood there until eventually I caught myself in the act of taking up position on the second bottom step. I walked off. Returned to St Pancras Station where I sat on the bench. No sight of the old woman. Nobody about; nothing at all. The rain had gone off. Maybe for good. I checked my money. The situation was not fine. I concentrated on working out a move for morning. And already there were signs of it; a vague alteration in the light and that odd sense of warmth the night can have for me was fast leaving.

Double or clear plus a tenner

Aside from the constant drone it was quiet in this section of the factory. In the smoke-area a group of men sat round a wooden table; a game of Solo was in progress. Although only four players could be directly involved the rest of the men gave it their utmost attention, each being positioned so that he could watch the cards of at least one of the four. The game was played quietly but laughter occurred, controlled, barely audible beyond the smoke-area. One of the players was a man by the name of Albert who smoked a pipe and had the habit of doffing and donning his bunnet all the time. While he was tapping a fresh shot of tobacco into the pipe bowl he was told to get a move on. It was his shout. He nodded to the youth sitting next to him who then lifted the cards and rapidly sorted through them, eventually saying: A bundle Albert, you're going for nine.

Albert grinned, exhaling smoke from the corner of his mouth he took the cards. So I'm to win nine am I, he said.

You're a certainty. Cant get beat.

Albert laughed at the other three players. You mob better be listening to this apprentice of mine.

He was answered by jeers, the game continued. About an hour later the sound of somebody whistling was heard and the Solo stopped abruptly; newspapers covered the cards and the men began chatting together, sitting back on their seats. The foreman entered, dressed in a white dustcoat he was holding a cardboard box from which he distributed the wage envelopes. While he did so he half smiled, Missed yous again eh. Ach well, one of these days, one of these days . . . As he turned to leave somebody asked if he had heard any news. Not a word, he shook his head. No even a whisper.

Without waiting for further comment the foreman left. The men examined the contents of the envelopes or thrust them unopened into their pockets. The conversation became general. Then a man who had been playing Solo rose to his feet, went a couple of paces and paused. It's no use kidding yourselves on, he said, if that order isnt in by now it'll never be fucking in.

The men were looking at him.

Redundancies, he continued; there's definitely going to be redundancies. So yous better get used to the idea.

Ach we knew it was coming, muttered Albert.

The man glanced at him: That's as maybe but they should've given us notice. Formal. It's no as if they've told us anything. All we're doing is guessing, and we shouldnt have to be fucking guessing.

They might no know for sure but, remarked somebody.

The man looked at him then left the smoke-area, shaking his head. A short silence followed. A small man spat on the floor and stroked it carefully with the heel of his boot. Another was lifting the newspapers from the cards on the table. He said, Come on, we'll finish the game.

One of the spectators quickly volunteered to take the place of the man who had mentioned redundancies, but the other spectators were no longer as attentive as before; within ten minutes the game ended. Some of those who had gone drifted back to the table. Albert and another player got up to make space for them and the former grunted, Yous and your fucking pontoons . . . He returned the pipe to his mouth and raised his bunnet.

The men still seated were grinning as they stacked columns of coins in front of them. Somebody was already shuffling the cards and he dealt one to each person to resolve who was to become the first banker. At the outset the stakes were restricted to a maximum of 50 pence but the banker would hold the initiative in this; later the figure was raised to £1 and eventually

153

limits were scrapped altogether. The deal was being held by Albert's apprentice. He had called the older man across and asked him to assist in posting the bets.

Collecting in the fucking money you mean. Albert grinned briefly. When the apprentice did not reply he went on to say, I hate this game — the sight of all the cash flying about goes to my head.

A player snorted, You're just scared to open your wages ya cunt ye.

A few people laughed.

Albert glared at the player: You trying to say I'm feart of the wife or something? aye well you're fucking right I am. Bringing out a box of matches he relighted his pipe and muttered, I'll enjoy taking in your dough anyway ya cunt.

The player chuckled. When he finished shuffling for the first round of his deal the apprentice got the previous banker to cut the cards then gazed round the table and said, Will yous space yourselves out a bit?

Christ, said somebody; always the fucking same when he gets the deal — we've got to arrange ourself out for his convenience.

Aye you're fucking right, replied the apprentice. I like to see what yous're doing with the cards.

That's my boy, grinned Albert.

The cards were dealt.

At 7.30 a.m. Albert, in company with other non players, had gone off to the washroom to clean up in preparation for clocking out. Some dayshift workers had already clocked in, two of them sitting in at pontoons although not having received their wages yet their stakes were minimal. The bank had been won and lost many times during the game. It had returned to the apprentice. And when a man told them it was 7.40 a.m. only he and two nightshift workers were left at the table. Lighting another cigarette he waited for them to evaluate the strength of their first cards and make their bets. One of them laid £15 down and the man who had told them the time said: Jesus Christ.

The apprentice won that bet and the rest. A round later and

someone called to say that the nightshift were waiting to clock out. He paused with the cards and glanced at the men. The one who had bet the £15 did not react but the other jumped up, grabbed his money and headed off to the washroom. See yous on Monday, he cried.

What d'you think? the apprentice asked the other man. Time we were moving?

Make the next yin the last.

He shrugged and dealt the cards. Moments later the dayshift chargehand came striding into the smoke-area and raising his arm he jerked the thumb of his right hand: Okay, out.

Last hand, muttered the man.

Last hand nothing. Come on, you'll get me fucking arrested.

The dayshift players had moved back from the table when their chargehand entered. Now when he saw the size of the bet between the two he shook his head, it was amounting to £40 this time. I dont believe this, he said, yous pair must be off your fucking head.

Surely we can finish it? said the apprentice.

No.

The other man glanced at him.

Stick your money out of sight, replied the chargehand and he left at once. Each retrieved his £20. The cards were still lying on the table. Deal them, the man whispered. And when he had received his two he asked for a twist, got a face card and was burst. He threw them down: Dirty bastard.

The apprentice took in the money without saying anything, and moved out from behind the table. The nightshift men had left the factory, Sitting on a bench he took off the boots and put on his shoes. The man was doing the same. Eventually he glanced at the apprentice: What about one last yin?

Waste of time man your luck's right out. Anyway, I'm still waiting for the score.

You're getting your score, dont worry.

I'm no worrying. He made to rise from the bench.

Last hand eh?

No point.

What d'you mean no point? the fucking money I've lost the night.

The apprentice shook his head; he dropped the cigarette he had been smoking and ground it on the floor.

Okay, the man continued, just a cut. One cut — double or clear . . . He stopped. A dayshift apprentice — younger than the card player by a couple of years — had come into the smoke-area at a rush, his face was red and he was out of breath. Christ, he said, yous two still here!

No, we're in the street. The man did not look at him.

The chargie's standing down at the gaffer's office.

He'll no say anything.

Aye he will — you dont know what he's like.

Course I fucking know what he's like, the man muttered. Then he added: Double or clear, eh? I mean surely you'll give me the chance of getting my dough back?

Fuck sake.

The dayshift apprentice had sat down on the bench to change shoes. He was taking note of the conversation. Eventually the man reached to collect the deck of cards and he passed them, he said: It's still your bank.

Ach, the apprentice nodded and took the cards. Double or clear then.

Plus a tenner, replied the man. Fifty to you if you win, okay?

The apprentice looked at him, he shuffled the cards rapidly and offered them to be cut. The man cut a low card and lost. He closed his eyes and did not speak. From the bench the other apprentice said: Was that for £50? Jesus Christ Almighty.

The two of them had their jerkins on as they walked down the length of the section and round to the clock-out. Throughout the area the machines were now in operation. A workman was bent over the flat part of one, wiping the metal with a paraffin soaked rag. He laughed: Did yous sleep in?

They ignored him. They did not look in the direction of the gaffer's office where the chargehand was standing; they carried on and out by the window of the timekeeper's office. Once onto the pavement of the street they halted. The man made as if to speak but sniffed instead, and remained silent. A group of women and children of school age were coming towards them. When they had gone by he said, I've no got the full fifty.

Fuck sake, I knew it.

I thought I did have, honest. I must've lost more than I thought.

Ach . . . The apprentice turned away but they stayed on the pavement for several seconds; he then took out his cigarettes and handed one to the man who brought out a lighter.

Okay if I owe you it?

The full fifty you mean?

The man nodded slightly, exhaling smoke.

Aye . . . the apprentice shrugged and they headed off in opposite directions.

A notebook to do with America

When he came out of the pub the snow was still falling, he paused to fix the bunnet properly on his head then crossed the large patch of waste ground to the building. It was the remnant of a tenement; much of the rest was lying around in disordered heaps. The close had been sealed off with a sheet of corrugated iron but the nails were removed from three of its sides and the man got in quite easily. He struck a match. The debris wasnt too bad. He lighted a cigarette before walking to the foot of the stair.

On the first floor each of the flats had had its door taken off. He passed quickly up to the second and chapped the only flat which had one. He chapped again. An interior door creaked, steps along the lobby floor, and soon an elderly woman peered at him. She would be about 10 years older than the man. She invited him in and he replied with a nod. Stepping over a big pile of laundry he followed her ben to the front room where two candles were flickering at opposite ends on the mantelpiece. She was indicating a dining chair: on it were a spectacle case and a notebook, and a grey soft hat and a maroon scarf; on the floor underneath stood a pair of brown shoes. The woman sat down on another dining chair which was set to one side of the fireplace. Not a bad fire was burning.

He glanced about for another chair. He stood by the mantelpiece. After several moments he sniffed and took out his cigarettes, handed her one, struck the match. Eventually he exhaled and said, No, I dont come down that much at all these days. Once or twice a week maybe. Too far. Too far to come for a pint. Miles away I'm living now. And these buses! Hell of a dear, bloody scandalous.

He sniffed again, rubbed his hands together briskly; he took the cigarette from his mouth and studied it. Aye, he said, hell of a dear. I still like to come back but . . . have a pint, see the old faces and that. Two buses though, one into town, then another I've got to get from there to here. Murder, the time it takes, you wouldnt credit it.

She had inhaled on her cigarette, tugged her coat round her shoulders, she exhaled into the fire and watched the two smokes mingle. Then she glanced at him to say: Will you be going to America?

What?

He said you would be.

Christ sake Mrs. He sniffed. How can I go to America? I cant go to America. He turned away from her and walked to the window where he gazed at the pub. It was a flat roofed kind of affair. Though outwardly modern the 19th century brickwork at the rear would reveal it to have been the ground floor of an ordinary three storey tenement until recently. A customer was entering. The bright light from inside showed a confusion of footprints in the snow at the doorway. Rubbing his hands again the man returned to stand by the mantelpiece. Freezing, he said, that fire . . . When she didnt reply he added: Will I get some wood or what?

He thought you would be going to America.

Aye . . . the man nodded.

He was wanting to go himself.

I know.

He would've.

The man made no answer but when she repeated the statement he muttered, No he wouldnt have, not now, he was too old, too old Mrs. That's how he asked me.

Aye but you're not going. She shook her head slightly, stared into the fire.

Christ sake it's no use talking about it like that, that was just talk; that was just talk. He just liked to talk to me about it down in the pub. Ach. Reaching into an interior pocket he brought out a halfbottle of whisky and uncapped it; he offered it to her before slugging a mouthful.

I waited for you, he said you'd come.

Aye.

He's ben in the kitchen. She leaned forwards to drop a portion of saliva onto the fireplace, picked a shred of tobacco from her lower lip. I covered him up.

The man nodded. A few moments later he said, Aye.

I'm making tea, she muttered. She rose from the chair and collected a saucepan and milkbottle of water from somewhere behind, and got tea from a packet on the mantelpiece. While she prepared the things she was saying, I had to lift him myself onto the table you know, it was a job.

He sighed. Christ sake Mrs . . . I wish you'd waited for me to come. When she finished the preparation he said, I'll away and see him.

No candles burned in the kitchen but it wasnt long before he could distinguish the body quite well; it was set properly on the table, entirely covered by a blanket. There was a pile of newspapers over at the gap where the sink used to be. He walked over to look out the window. The pub was not visible from this side of this building. He raised his bunnet and wiped his brow; he went back to the table and cleared his throat as if getting ready to speak but instead he lifted the blanket and looked at the face. An old face, years older than the woman probably. He continued looking until a length of ash fell from his cigarette. He blew quickly to scatter it, drew the blanket into its former place.

He shut the door behind him.

Aye . . . he sighed. Some minutes passed. He took out the halfbottle and after offering her it he sipped some himself. When the bubbles were forming and bursting in the saucepan he sniffed and touched the peak of his bunnet. I think I'll just go down the road, he said.

Are you taking the notebook?

Eh aye, he sniffed again, if you dont mind.

The woman nodded and he got the notebook. He shook his head when she indicated the other items and went away soon after.

The hitchhiker

It was a terrible night. From where we were passing the loch lay hidden in the mist and drenching rain. We followed the bend leading round and down towards the village. Each of us held an empty cardboard box above his head. The barman had given them to us, but though they were saturated they were definitely better than nothing. We had been trudging in silence. When we arrived at the bridge over the burn Chas said, There's your hitchhiker.

I glanced up, saw her standing by the gate into one of the small cottages. She appeared to be hesitating. But she went on in, and chapped at the door. A light came on and a youngish woman answered, she shook her head, pointed along the road. The three of us had passed beyond the gate. About 30 yards on I turned to look back, in time to see her entering the path up to the door of another cottage. A man answered and shut the door immediately. The girl was standing there staring up at the window above the door; the porchlight was switched off. Two huge rucksacks strapped onto her back and about her shoulders and when she was walking from the cottage she seemed bent under their weight. Young lassie like that, muttered Sammy. She shouldnt be walking the streets on a night like this.

Aye, said Chas, but she doesnt look as if she's got anywhere to go. It's a while since we saw her.

I nodded. I thought she'd have had a lift by this time. Soaked as well, I said. Look at her.

She's no the only one that's soaked, replied Sammy. Come on, let's move.

Wait a minute, Christ sake.

The girl had noticed us watching her, she quickened her pace in the opposite direction. Sammy said: She's feart.

What?

He grinned at me, indicating the cardboard boxes. The three of us standing gaping at her! what d'you expect son? Sammy paused: If she was my lassie . . . Naw, she shouldnt be out on a night like this.

Not her fault she cant get a lift.

Single lassies shoudnt go hitching on their tod.

Sammy's right, grinned Chas. No with bastards like us going about.

Come on yous pair . . . Sammy was already walking away: Catch pneumonia hanging about in weather like this.

Just a minute, wait till we see what happens.

He paused, glowering at me and grunting unintelligibly. Meanwhile the girl was in chapping on the door of the next cottage. The person who answered gestured along the road in our direction; but once the door had closed she gazed at us in a defiant way and carried on in the opposite direction.

Dirty bastards, I shook my head, not letting her in.

Chas laughed: I'd let her in in a minute.

Away you ya manky swine ye, cried Sammy. His eyebrows rose when he added, Still — she's got a nice wee arse on her.

These specs of yours must have Xray lenses to see through that anorak she's wearing.

Sammy grinned: Once you reach my age son . . .

Bet you she's a foreigner, said Chas.

A certainty, I nodded.

The girl had just about disappeared into the mist. She crossed over the bridge and I could no longer distinguish her. And a moment later the older man was saying: Right then I'm off.

Chas agreed, Might as well.

The pair of them continued on. I strode after them. Heh Sammy, can the lassie stay the night with us?

Dont be daft son.

How no?

No room.

There is, just about.

Nonsense.

Christ sake Sammy how would you like to be kipping in a ditch on a night like this, eh? fuck sake, no joke man I'm telling you.

God love us son; sharing a caravan with the three of us! you kidding? Anyhow, the lassie herself'd never wear it.

I'll go and tell her it'll be okay but. I mean she can have my bunk, I'll kip on the floor.

Chas was grinning. Sammy shook his head, he muttered: Goodsafuckingmaritans, I dont know what it is with yous at all.

Ach come on.

Sammy grunted: What d'you say Chas?

Nothing to do with me, he grinned.

Good on you Chas, I said.

Ah! Sammy shook his head: The lassie'll never wear it.

We'll see.

I passed him the carry-out of beer I had been holding and ran back and across the bridge but when I saw her I slowed down. She had stopped to shrug the rucksacks up more firmly on her shoulders. A few paces on and she stopped again. I caught up to her and said, Hello, but she ignored me. She continued walking.

Hello.

She halted. To see me she twisted her body to the side, she was raging. Glaring at me.

Have you no place to stay? I said.

She hoisted the rucksacks up and turned away, going as fast as she could. I went after her. She was really angry. Before I got my mouth open she stopped and yelled: What.

Have you not got a place for the night?

Pardon . . . She glanced along the road as she said this but there was nobody else in sight. Never anybody in sight in this place, right out in the middle of the wilds it was.

Dont worry. It's okay. You need a place for the night. A house, a place out the rain — eh?

What?

A place to stay the night?

You know?

Hotel, there's a hotel.

Yes yes yes hotel, hotel. She shrugged: It is too much. She looked at me directly and said, Please — I go.

Listen a minute; you can come back to our place. I have place.

I . . . do not understand.

You can come to our place, it's okay, a caravan. Better than hanging about here getting soaked.

She pointed at my chest: You stay?

Aye, yes, I stay. Caravan.

No! And off she trudged.

I went after her. Listen it's okay, no bother — it's not just me. Two friends, the three of us, it's not . . . I mean it's okay, it'll be alright, honest.

She turned on me, raging. What a face. She cried: 1 2 3 . . . And tapped the numbers out on her fingers. 1 2 3, she cried. All man and me.

She tapped 1 finger to her temple and went on her way without hesitation. At the lane which led up to the more modern cottages used by the forestry workers she paused for an instant, then continued along it and out of sight.

Inside the caravan Chas had opened a can of lager for me while I was finishing drying my hair. Both he and Sammy were already under the blankets but they were sitting up, sipping lager and smoking. The rain battered the sides and the roof and the windows of the caravan.

Chas was saying: Did you manage to get through to her but?

Get through to her! Course I didnt get fucking through to her — thought I was going to rape her or something.

Hell of a blow to your ego son, eh! Sammy grinned.

Fuck my ego. Tell you one thing, I'll never sleep the night.

Aye you will, said Chas. You get used to it.

You never get used to it. Never mind but, Sammy chuckled,

165

you can have a chug when we're asleep . . . He laid the can of beer on the floor next to his bunk and wiped his lips with his wrist; he took another cigarette from his packet and lighted it from the dowp-end of the one he had been smoking. He was still chuckling as he said: Mind fine when I was down in Doncaster . . .

Fuck Doncaster.

Chas laughed. Never mind him Sammy — let's hear it.

Naw, better no. Sammy smiled, Wouldnt be fair to the boy.

When I had dried my feet I walked into the kitchenette to hang up the towel. The top section of the window was open. I closed it. If anything the rain seemed to be getting heavier. And back in the main area Chas said: She'll be swimming out there.

Thanks, I said.

Thanks! Sammy snorted, You'd think it was him swimming!

I drank a mouthful of lager, sat down at the foot of my bunk, and lifted the cigarette one of them had left for me. Chas tossed me the matches. A·few·moments passed before Sammy muttered: Aye, just a pity you never thought to tell her about next door.

I looked at him.

The sparks, he said, they're not here tonight. Had to go back down to Glasgow for some reason.

What?

I'm no sure, I think they needed a bit of cable or something.

Jesus Christ! How in the name of fuck could you no've told me already ya stupid auld . . . I was grabbing my socks and my boots.

Sammy had begun laughing. I forgot son honest, I forgot, I forgot, honest.

Chas was also laughing. The two of them, sitting spluttering over their lager. Fine pair of mates yous are, I told them. Eh! Fuck sake, never've signed on by Christ if I'd known about yous two bastarn comedians. Aye, no wonder they keep dumping yous out in the wilds to work.

Will you listen to this boy? Sammy was chortling.

And Chas yelling: Aye, and me about to lend him my duffel coat as well.

Keeping to the grass verge at the side of the track I walked quickly along from the small group of caravans. The centre of the track was bogging. It was always bogging. Even during the short heatwave of the previous week it was bogging. Plastered in animal shit. Cows and sheep and hens, even a couple of skinny goats, they all trooped down here from the flearidden farm a couple of fields away. By the time I got to the road my boots and the bottoms of my jeans were in a hell of a mess. I headed along to the village. Village by Christ — half a dozen cottages and a general store cum post office and the bastards called it a village. Not even a boozer. You had to trek another couple of miles further on to a hotel if you wanted a pint.

Over the bridge I went up the lane to the modern cottages. Although the mist had lifted a bit it was black night but it wasnt too bad, the occasional porchlight having been left on. Where the lane ended I turned back. If she was here she was either sheltering, or hiding.

Round the bend I continued in the direction of the hotel. The rain had definitely lessened, moonlight was glinting on the waters of the loch. I saw her standing at a wee wall next to the carpark entrance, she was with a very old man who was dressed in yellow oilskins, a small yap of a terrier darted about in the weeds at the side of the road. My approach had been noted. The girl finished muttering something to him, and he nodded. She made a movement of some kind, her face had tightened; she stared in the direction of the loch.

Well, I said. Has she not got a place yet?

What was that? The old man leaning to hear me.

I said has she not got a place yet, the lassie, she was looking for a place.

O aye aye, a place.

Aye, a place, has she got one yet?

He waited a moment before shaking his head, and while he

half gazed away from me he was saying: I've been telling her try up at Mrs Taylor's house.

Were you?

Aye, aye I was telling her to try there. You know Mrs Taylor's I would think.

Naw, I dont, I dont at all.

Is that right . . . he had glanced at me. You dont know her house then, aye, aye. No, I dont think she'd have any rooms at this time of night. Mrs Taylor, he shook his head. A queer woman that.

The girl turned her head, she was gazing in through the carpark entrance. But her gaze had included me in its manoeuvre. Look, I told the old man. I'm living on that wee caravan site along past the village. There's a spare one next to where I am. Tell her she'd be alright in there for the night.

He looked at me.

Look it's empty, an empty caravan, she'll be on her tod, nothing to worry about for Christ sake.

The old man paused then stepped the paces to begin chattering to her in her own language. Eventually she nodded, without speaking. She'll go, he said to me.

I told him to tell her I would carry her rucksacks if she wanted. But she shook her head. He shrugged, and the two of us watched her hitch them up onto her shoulders; then she spoke very seriously with him, he smiled and patted her arm. And she was off.

I nodded to him and followed.

She stared directly in front of her thick hiking boots. We passed over the bridge and on to the turnoff for the site. A rumble from the mountains across the loch was followed by a strike of lightning that brightened the length of the bogging track. A crack of thunder. Look, I said, I might as well get a hold of your rucksacks along here, it's hell of a muddy . . . I pointed to the rucksacks indicating I should carry them. I helped them from her. She swung them down and I put one over each of my shoulders. Setting off on the grass verge I then heard her coming splashing along in the middle of the bog, not bothering at all.

The light was out in our caravan. I showed her to the one next, and opened the door for her, standing back to let her enter but she waved me inside first. Dumping the rucksacks on the floor of the kitchenette we went into the main area, it was the same size as the one shared by the three of us. These caravans were only really meant for two people. A stale smell of socks and sweat about the place, but it was fine apart from this, fairly tidy; the sparks must have given it a going over before returning to Glasgow, and they had taken all their gear with them.

The girl had her arms folded and her shoulders hunched, as if she had recently shivered. She stood with her back to the built-in wardrobe. I nodded and said: I'll be back in a minute.

Chas was snoring. I could see the red glow from Sammy's cigarette. He always had trouble getting to sleep unless drunk; this evening we'd only had 4 or 5 pints each over a period of maybe 3 hours. He said: I heard yous.

Any tea bags?

My jacket pocket.

I also collected two cups and the tin of condensed milk from the cupboard in the kitchenette. It's still teeming down out there, I whispered.

Aye.

She's soaked through. I hesitated, Okay then Sammy — goodnight.

Goodnight son.

I chapped on the door before entering. She was now sitting on a bunk but still wore both her anorak and her hiking boots, her hands thrust deep inside the anorak pockets. When I had made the tea she held the cupful in both hands. No food, I said.

Pardon?

Food, I've no food.

Ah. Yes . . . She placed the tea on the floor, drew a rucksack to her, unzipped it and brought out a plastic container from which she handed me a sandwich. Then she closed the container without taking one for herself.

After a few sips of tea she said, Tea very good.

Aye, you cant beat it.

She looked at me.

The tea, I said, you cant beat it — very very good.

Yes.

She refused a cigarette and when I had my own smoking she asked: You work.

Aye, yes.

Not stay? She gestured at the window. The rain pounding at it.

Naw, not stay. I grinned: I stay in Glasgow.

Ah, she nodded, my friend is Glasgow.

Great place Glasgow. You like it?

Glasgow very good.

Great stuff, have another cup of tea immediately.

She looked at me.

Tea — more tea?

She shook her head. You ah . . . You . . . She continued in french and finished with a shrug: I cannot say this with english.

I shrugged as well and as soon as I had swallowed the last of the tea I rose to put the cups on the draining board at the sink. The girl said, You go now.

I smiled. I go now.

Yes.

In the morning, tomorrow morning I'll be here.

Yes.

I paused at the door.

She half smiled. Tired, tired tired tired.

I nodded and said, Goodnight.

Both of them were washed and ready to leave when I woke up next morning. When Sammy was out of earshot I asked Chas if he thought he would mind if I was a bit late in. Ask him and see, was the reply. Sammy scratched his head when I did. He said: Okay but dont be all morning. I pulled the blankets up to my chin but as soon as I heard the car engine revving I got out of the bunk and dressed. Brushed my teeth, shaved.

Outside it was dry, fresh, a clear morning in June. Across the loch puffy clouds round the Ben. In the hotel bar the previous night Sammy had forecast a return of the warm weather, and it looked like he was going to be right. There was no reply when I chapped the door. I chapped again and went inside. Clothes strewn about the place, as if she had unpacked every last item. And her smell was here now.

She was sleeping on her side, facing into the wall. I stepped back out and chapped the door loudly. Rustling sounds. I clicked the door open.

No!

It's me.

No!

I remained with my hand on the door knob.

Come!

Her hair rumpled, a pair of jeans and a Tshirt she was wearing, eyes almost closed; she moved about picking things up off the floor and folding them away into the rucksacks; so much stuff lying it seemed odds against the rucksacks being able to take it all. I filled the kettle and shoved it on to boil the water. She looked up: Tea?

Aye, yes, tea.

Your friends?

Work.

Ah.

She stopped clearing up, she yawned while sitting down on the bunk with her back to the wall and her legs drawn up, resting her elbows on her knees. She gazed over her shoulder, out of the window, murmuring to herself in french.

You sleep okay?

Yes, she replied.

She had the plastic container out, the sandwiches ready, when I came back with the tea.

I said, It's a great morning outside, really great. The morning, outside, the weather, really beautiful.

Ah, yes . . . She looked out of the window again and spoke in french, she shrugged.

Tea good?

Very very good, she smiled. She passed me the plastic container.

Fine sandwiches, I told her. What kind of stuff is this?

Pardon?

I parted the 2 slices of bread.

O. Sausage. You like?

It's good.

Yes. Suddenly she laughed, she laughed and held up the sandwich she was eating: In Glasgow piece — a piece. Yes?

Christ.

She laughed again, flicking the hair from her face: My friend in Glasgow she say peez, geez peez pleez.

That's right geeza piece, I grinned. Heh, more tea? fancy some more tea?

She nodded.

At the turnoff for the Mallaig Road we shook hands in a solemn sort of way, and she headed along in that direction, her gaze to where the boots were taking her. I watched until she reached the first bend on the road. She hadnt looked back at all.

When I banged out the signal the hammering halted and I crawled through the short narrow tunnel into the big chlorine tank we were relining. I climbed the scaffolding. The two of them were now sitting on the edge of the platform, their legs dangling over, having a smoke. Without speaking I got the working gear on, pulled the safety-helmet, the goggles and the breathing mask into their right positions about my head. While tugging the sweatband down to my brow a loud snort came from Sammy, and he said: Looks like he's decided not to speak.

Aye, said Chas.

Waiting for us to ask I suppose.

Must be.

God love us.

172

A moment later Chas glanced at me: Well?

Well what?

Well?

Well well well.

Hh, Christ.

Ach never bother with him, grunted Sammy.

But Chas said: Did you or didnt you?

What? What d'you mean?

Did you or fucking didnt you?

Did I or didnt I what?

Sammy sighed: Aye or naw, that's all he's asking.

Is it? I laughed.

Orange bastard, muttered Sammy.

So you did then, Chas asked.

Did what?

Ah fuck off.

What's up.

What's up! Chas said, Are you going to tell us? aye or naw!

I had a look at the hammer to make sure it was properly adjusted onto the pressurised air-hose, then got myself a chisel. By the way, I said, thanks for bringing my gear up from below, makes a difference having good mates on a job like this.

Sammy gazed at me. He said to Chas: You wouldnt credit it — look at him, he's not going to tell us anything right enough. Tell you something for nothing Chas it's the last time the cunt'll even smell one of these tea bags of mine.

That goes for my duffel coat, grunted Chas.

I fixed the chisel into the nozzle of the hammer, and began whistling.

Fuck off, cried Chas.

Ach. Never bother, muttered Sammy, never bother. Who's interested anyhow!

I slung the hammer across my shoulder, tugging the airhose across to the place I had stopped at the day before. Both of them were watching me. I winked before pulling the goggles down over my eyes, triggered off the hammer.

173

Wee horrors

The backcourt was thick with rubbish as usual. What a mess. I
never like thinking about the state it used to get into. As soon as
a family flitted out to the new home all the weans were in and
dragging off the abandoned furnishings & fittings, most of
which they dumped. Plus with the demolition work going on
you were getting piles of mortar and old brickwork everywhere.
A lot of folk thought the worst kind of rubbish was the soft
goods, the mattresses and dirty clothing left behind by the
ragmen. Fleas were the problem. It seemed like every night of
the week we were having to root them out once the weans came
in. Both breeds we were catching, the big yins and the wee yins,
the dark and the rusty brown. The pest-control went round
from door to door. Useless. The only answer was keeping the
weans inside but ours were too old for that. Having visitors in
the house was an ordeal, trying to listen to what they were
saying while watching for the first signs of scratching. Then last
thing at night, before getting into bed, me and the wife had to
make a point of checking through our own stuff. Apart from
that there was little to be done about it. We did warn the weans
but it was useless. Turn your back and they were off downstairs
to play at wee houses, dressing-up in the clothes and bouncing
on the mattresses till all you were left hoping was they would
knock the stuffing out the fleas. Some chance. You have to
drown the cunts or burn them. A few people get the knack of
crushing them between thumbnail and forefinger but I could
never master that. Anyway, fleas have got nothing to do with
this. I was down in the backcourt to shout my pair up for their

tea. The woman up the next close had told me they were all involved in some new den they had built and if I saw hers while I was at it I was to send them up right away. The weans were always making dens. It could be funny to see. You looked out the window and saw what you thought was a pile of rubble and maybe a sheet of tarpaulin stuck on the top. Take another look and you might see a wee head poking out, then another, and another, till finally maybe ten of them were standing there, thinking the coast was clear. But on this occasion I couldnt see a thing. I checked out most of the possibilities. Nothing. No signs of them anywhere. And it was quiet as well. Normally you would've at least heard a couple of squeaks. I tramped about for a time, retracing my steps and so on. I was not too worried. It would have been different if only my pair was missing but there was no sight nor sound of any description. And I was having to start considering the dunnies. This is where I got annoyed. I've always hated dunnies — pitchblack and that smell of charred rubbish, the broken glass, these things your shoes nudge against. Terrible. Then if you're in one and pause a moment there's this silence forcing you to listen. Really bad. I had to go down but. In the second one I tried I found some of the older mob, sitting in a kind of circle round two candles. They heard me come and I knew they had shifted something out of sight, but they recognised me okay and one of the lassies told me she had seen a couple of weans sneaking across to Greegor's. I was really angry at this. I had told them umpteen times never to go there. By rights the place should've got knocked down months ago but progress was being blocked for some reason I dont know, and now the squatters and a couple of the girls were in through the barricading. If you looked over late at night you could see the candle glow at the windows and during the day you were getting the cars crawling along near the pavement. It was hopeless. I went across. Once upon a time a grocer had a shop in the close and this had something to do with how it got called Greegor's. Judging from the smell of food he was still in business. At first I thought it was coming from up the close but the nearer I got I could tell it was coming from the dunny. Down I went. Being a corner block there were a good few twists and turns from the entrance lobby and I was having to go carefully. It felt like planks of wood I was walking on. Then the sounds. A kind of sizzling — making you think of a piece of fucking silverside in the oven, these crackling noises when the juice spurts out. Jesus christ. I shouted the names of my pair. The sound of feet scuffling. I turned a corner and got a hell of a shock — a woman standing in a doorway. Her face wasnt easy to see because of the light from behind her. Then a man appeared. He began nodding away with a daft smile on his face. I recognised them. Wineys. They had been dossing about the area for the past while. Even the face she had told a story, white with red blotches, eyes always seeming to water. She walked in this queer kind of stiff shuffle, her shoes flapping. When she stepped back from the doorway she drew the cuff of her coat sleeve across her mouth. The man was still giving his daft smiles. I followed. Inside the room all the weans were gathered round the middle of the floor. Sheets of newspaper had been spread about. I spotted my pair immediately — scared out their wits at seeing me. I just looked at them. Over at the fireplace a big fire was going, not actually in the fireplace, set to about a yard in front. The spit was fashioned above it and a wee boy stood there, he must've been rotating the fucking thing. Three lumps of meat sizzled away and just to the side were a few cooked bits lined in a row. I hadnt noticed the woman walk across but then she was there and making a show of turning the contraption just so I would know she wasnt giving a fuck about me being there. And him — still smiling, then beginning to make movements as if he wanted to demonstrate how it all worked. He was pointing out a row of raw lumps on the mantelpiece and then reaching for a knife with a thin blade. I shook my head, jesus christ right enough. I grabbed for my pair, yelling at the rest of the weans to get up that effing stair at once.

le jouer

Him with the long face and that conical hat sitting there with the clay pipe stuck in his mouth, the widower: he enters this *café* around 7 every evening with a nod to the barman, a quick look to ensure his chair and table are vacant; though in a place as quiet as this anything else seems out of the question. Lurking about at the rear of the table is a wee black & white dog that finally settles into a prone position in the shadows by the wall beneath the grimy mirror. On putting the tall bottle of wine and the two glasses down onto the table, the widower has tugged this huge coloured handkerchief from his right jacket pocket, and into it has given a muffled honk; and sniffed while stuffing it back out of sight. Several moments on he is glancing across at the clock on the gantry and taking the handkerchief out once more, to wipe at his nostrils.

The door has opened.

That younger man — him with the upturned brim on his hat — has walked in, hands in coat pockets; and a half twitch of the head by way of greeting the barman; and a half rise of the eyebrows on seeing the widower's glance at the clock. A deck of cards he lifts from the bar *en route* to the empty seat facing the widower. With a slow yawn the dog lowers its head, closes its eyes, reverting into its prone position. While the wine is being

177

poured by one the other is shuffling to deal methodically, ten cards apiece.

Later, him with the conical hat will rise and knock the bowl of the clay pipe against the heel of his right boot and without so much as a grunt will head for the exit followed by the wee black & white dog; and this dog must dodge smartly to get out before the door shuts on it.

That younger man will have refilled his own glass and will then gather up the cards and, as he is shuffling, he will be gazing round the interior of the room: but the only person present apart from the barman will be *Paul Cézanne*: and so he will continue to shuffle the cards for a period, before setting out the first game of *solitaire* while half wondering if his kids are behaving themselves.

Roofsliding[1]

The tenement building upon which the practice occurs is of the three storey variety. A section of roof bounded on both sides by a row of chimney stacks is favoured. No reason is known as to why this particular section should be preferred to another. Certain members of the group participating are thought to reside outwith this actual building though none is a stranger to the district. *Roofsliding*, as it is termed, can take place more than once per week and will always do so during a weekday mid morning. As to the season of the year, this is unimportant; dry days, however, being much sought after.

The men arise in single file from out of the rectangular skylight. They walk along the peak of the roof ensuring that one foot is settling on either side of the jointure which is bevelled in design, the angle at the peak representing some 80 degrees. During the walk slates have been known to break loose from their fixtures and if bypassing the gutter will topple over the edge of the building to land on the pavement far below. To offset any danger to the public a boy can always be seen on the opposite pavement, from where he will give warning to the pedestrians.

1 This account has been taken more or less verbatim from a pamphlet entitled *Within Our City Slums*; it belongs to the chapter headed 'Curious practices of the Glaswegian'. The pamphlet was published in 1932 but is still available in a few 2nd hand bookshops in the south of England.

When the men, sometime designated *roofsliders*, have assembled along the peak they will lower themselves to a sitting posture on the jointure, the legs being outstretched flatly upon the sloped roof. They face to the front of the building. *Roofsliding* will now commence. The feet push forward until the posterior moves off from the jointure onto the roof itself, the process continuing until the body as a whole lies prone on the gradient at which point momentum is effected.

Whether a man 'slides' with arms firmly aligned to the trunk, or akimbo, or indeed lying loosely to the sides, would appear to be a function of the number of individuals engaged in the activity at any given period (as many as 32 are said to have participated on occasion). Legs are, however, kept tightly shut. When the feet come to rest on the gutter *roofsliding* halts at once and the order in which members finish plays no part in the practice.

A due pause will now occur. Afterwards the men manoeuvre themselves inch by inch along the edge of the roof while yet seeming to maintain the prone position. Their goal, the line of chimney stacks that stand up right to the northside of the section. From here the men make their way up to the jointure on hands and knees. It is worth noting that they do so by way of the *outside*, unwilling, it would appear, to hazard even the slightest damage to the 'sliding' section that is bounded between here and the line of chimney stacks to the southside. When all have gathered on the jointure once again they will be seated to face the rear of the building. Now and now only shall conversation be entered upon. For up until this period not a man amongst them shall have spoken (since arrival by way of the skylight).

At present a ruddy complexioned chap in his 44th year is the 'elder statesman' of the *roofsliders*. Although the ages do vary within the group no youth shall be admitted who has yet to attain his 14th birthday. On the question of alcohol members are rightly severe, for not only would the 'wrong doer' be at mortal risk, so too would the lives of each individual.

As a phenomenon there can be no doubt as to the curious nature of the practice of *roofsliding*. Further observation might well yield fruits.

Not not while the giro

say not talkin about
not analysin nuthin
is if not not

Tom Leonard, *Breathe deep and regular with it*

of tea so I can really enjoy this 2nd last smoke which will be very
very strong which is of course why I drink tea with it in a sense
to counteract the harm it must do my inners. Not that tea cures
cancer poisoning or even guards against nicotine — helps
unclog my mouth a little. Maybe it doesnt. My mouth tastes
bad. Hot and kind of squelchy. I am smoking too much old
tobacco. 2nd hand tobacco is stiff, is burnt ochre in colour and
you really shudder before spluttering on the 1st drag. But this is
supposed to relieve the craving for longer periods. Maybe it
does. It makes no difference anyway, you still smoke them 1
after the other because what happens if you suddenly come into
a few quid or fresh tobacco — you cant smoke 2nd hand stuff
with the cashinhand and there isnt much chance of donating it
to fucking charity. So you smoke rapidly. I do — even with
fresh tobacco.

But though the tea is gone I can still enjoy the long smoke. A
simple enjoyment, and without guilt. I am wasting time. I am to
perambulate to a distant broo. I shall go. I always go. No
excuse now it has gone. And it may be my day for the spotcheck
at the counter. Rain pours heavily. My coat is in the fashion of
yesteryear but I am wearing it. How comes this coat to be with
me yet. Not a question although it bears reflecting upon at
some later date. Women may have something to do with it.
Probably not, that cannot be correct. Anyway, it has nothing to
do with anything.

I set myself small tasks, ordeals; for instance: Come on ya bastard ye and smoke your last, then see how your so-called will fucking power stands up. Eh! Naw, you wont do that. Of course I wont, but such thoughts often occur. I may or may not smoke it. And if it does come down to will power how the hell can I honestly say I have any — when circumstances are as they are. Could begin smacking of self pity shortly if this last continues. No, yesteryear's coat is not my style. Imitation Crombies are unbecoming these days, particularly the kind with narrow lapels. This shrewd man I occasionally have dealings with refused said coat on the grounds of said lapels rendering the coat an undesired object by those who frequent said man's premises. Yet I would have reckoned most purchasers of 2nd hand clothing to be wholly unaware of fashions current or olden. But I have faith in him. He does fine. Pawnshops could be nationalized. What a shock for the small-trader. What next that's what we'd like to know, the corner bloody shop I suppose. Here that's not my line of thought at all. Honest to god, right hand up that the relative strength of the freethinkers is neither here nor there. All we ask is to play up and play the game. Come on you lot, shake hands etcetera. Jesus what is this at all. Fuck all to do with perambulations to the broo.

Last smoke between my lips, right then. Fire flicked off, the last colour gone from the bar. Bastarn rain. The Imitation Crombie. And when I look at myself in the mirror I can at least blow smoke in my face. Also desperately needing a pish. Been holding it in for ages by the feel of things. Urinary infections too, they are caused by failing to empty the bladder completely ie. cutting a long pish short and not what's the word — flicking the chopper up and down to get rid of the drips. Particularly if one chances to be uncircumcised. Not at all.

In fact I live in a single bedsitter with sole use of confined kitchenette whose shelves are presently idle. My complexion could be termed grey. As though he hadnt washed for a month your worship. Teeth not so good. Beard a 6 dayer and of all unwashed colours. Shoes suede and stained by dripping. Dripping! The jeans could be fashionable without the Imitation Crombie. Last smoke finished already by christ. Smile. Yes. Hullo. Walk to door. Back to collect the sign-on card from its safe place. I shall be striding through a downpour.

Back from the broo and debating whether I am a headcase after all and this has nothing to do with my ambling in the rain. A neighbour has left a child by my side and gone off to the launderette. An 18 month old child and frankly an imposition. I am not overly fond of children. And this one is totally indifferent to me. The yes I delivered to the neighbour was typically false. She knew fine well but paid no attention. Perhaps she dislikes me intensely. Her husband and I detest each other. In my opinion his thoughts are irrelevant yet he persists in attempting to gain my heed. He fails. My eyes glaze but he seems unaware. Yet his wife appreciates my position and this is important since I can perhaps sleep with her if she sides with me or has any thoughts on the subject of him in relation to me or vice versa. Hell of a boring. I am not particularly attracted to her. A massive woman. I dont care. My vanities lie in other fields. Though at 30 years of age one's hand is insufficient and to be honest again my hand is more or less unused in regard to sexual relief. I rely on the odd wet dream, the odd chance acquaintance, male or female it makes no difference yet either has advantages.

Today the streets were crowded as was the broo. Many elderly women were out shopping and why they viewed me with suspicion is beyond me. I am the kind of fellow who gets belted by umbrellas for the barging of so-called 'infirm' pensioners while boarding omnibuses. Nonsense. I am polite. It is possible the Imitation Crombie brushes their shoulders or something in passing but the coat is far too wide for me and if it bumps against anything is liable to cave in rather than knock a body flying. Then again, I rarely wear the garment on buses. Perhaps they think I'm trying to lift their purses or provisions. You never know. If an orange for example dropped from a bag and rolled in my direction I would be reluctant to hand it back to its rightful owner. I steal. In supermarkets I lift flat items such as cheese and other articles. Last week, having allowed the father of the screaming infant to buy me beer in return for my ear, I got a large ashtray and two pint glasses and would have got more but that I lacked the Imitation Crombie. I do not get captured. I got shoved into jail a long time ago but not for stealing cheese. Much worse. Although I am an obviously suspicious character I never get searched. No more.

My shoes lie by the fire, my socks lie on its top. Steam rises. Stomach rumbles. I shall dine with the parents. No scruples on this kind of poncing. This angers the father as does my inability to acquire paid employment. He believes I am not trying, maintains there must be something. And while the mother accepts the prevailing situation she is apt to point out my previous job experience. I have worked at many things. I seldom stay for any length of time in a job because I cannot. Possibly I am a hopeless case.

I talk not at all, am confined to quarters, have no friends. I often refer to persons as friends in order to beg more easily from said persons in order that I may be the less guilty. Not that guilt affects me. It affects my landlord. He climbs the stairs whenever he is unwelcome elsewhere. He is a nyaff, yet often threatens to remove me from the premises under the mis-apprehension I would not resort to violence. He mentions the mother of this infant in lewd terms but I shall have none of it. Maybe he is a secret child molester. I might spread rumours to pass the time. But no, the infant is too wee. Perhaps I am a latent molester for even considering that. Below me dwells the Mrs. Soinson, she has no children and appears unaware of my existence. I have thought of bumping into her and saying, Can I watch your television.

Not Not While The Giro

Aye, of course I'll keep the kid for another bastarn half hour. Good christ this is pathetic. The damn parent has to go further messages. Too wet to trail one's offspring. I could hardly reply for rage and noises from the belly and sweet odours from the room of a certain new tenant whom I have yet to clap eyes upon though I hear she is a young lady, a student no doubt, with middle class admirers or fervent working class ones or even upper class yacht drivers. I cannot be expected to compete with that sort of opposition. I shall probably flash her a weary kind of ironic grin that will strike her to the very marrow and gain all her pity/sympathy/respect for a brave but misguided soul. What sort of pish is this at all. Fuck sake I refuse to contemplate further on it although I only got lost in some train of thought and never for one moment contemplated a bastarn thing. I day dream frequently.

This infant sleeps on the floor in an awkward position and could conceivably suffocate but I wont rouse her. The worst could not happen with me here. Scream the fucking place down if I woke her up.

I am fed up with this business. Always my own fault with the terrible false yesses I toss around at random. Why can I not give an honest no like other people. The same last time. I watched the infant all Friday night while the parents were off for a few jars to some pub uptown where this country & western songster performs to astonishing acclaim. Now why songster and not singer. Anyway, they returned home with a ½ bottle of whisky and a couple of cans of lager so it wasnt too bad. This country & western stuff isnt as awful as people say yet there are too many tales of lost loves and horses for my liking although I admit to enjoying a good weepy now and then unless recovering from a hangover in which case — in which case . . . Christ, I may imagine things more than most but surely the mother — whom for the sake of identity I'll hereon refer to as Greta. And I might as well call him Percy since it is the worst I can think of at present — displayed her thigh on purpose. This is a genuine question. If I decide on some sort of action I must be absolutely sure of my ground, not be misled into thinking one thing to be true when in fact the other thing is the case. What. O jesus I have too many problems to concentrate on last week and the rest of it. Who the hell cares. I do. I do, I wish to screw her, be with her in bed for a lengthy period.

Oxtail soup and insufficient bread which lay on a cracked plate. Brought on a tray. Maybe she cant trust herself alone with me. Hard to believe she returned to lunch off similar fare below. I cant help feeling nobody would offer someone soup under the title of 'lunch' without prior explanation. Tea did of course follow but no further bread. I did not borrow from her. I wanted to. I should have. It was necessary. I somehow expected her to perceive my plight and suggest I accept a minor sum to tide me over, but no. I once tried old Percy for a fiver on his wages day. He looked at me as if I was daft. Five quid. A miserable five. Lend money and lose friends was his comment. Friends by christ.

Sucked my thumb to taste the nicotine. A salty sandish flavour. Perhaps not. In the good old days I could have raked the coal embers for cigarette ends. Wet pavements. I am in a bad way — even saying I am in a bad way. 3.30 in the afternoon this approximate Thursday. I have until Saturday morning to starve to death though I wont. I shall make it no bother. The postman comes at 8.20 — 7.50 on Saturdays but the bastarn postoffice opens not until 9.00 and often 9.05 though they deny it.

I refuse to remain here this evening. I will go beg in some pub where folk know me. In the past I have starved till the day before payday then tapped a handful on the strength of it and ... christ in the early days I got a tenner once or twice and blew the lot and by the time I had repaid this and reached the Saturday late night I was left with thirty bob to get me through the rest of the week ie. the following 7 days. Bad bad. Waking in the morning and trying to slip back into slumber blotting out the harsh truth but it never works and there you are wide awake and aware and jesus it is bad. Suicide can be contemplated. Alright. I might have contemplated it. Or maybe I only imagined it, I mean seriously considered it. Or even simply and without the seriously. In other words I didnt contemplate suicide at all. I probably regarded the circumstances as being ideal. Yet in my opinion

No more of this shite. But borrowing large sums knowing they have to be repaid and the effects etc must have something to do with the deathwish. I refuse to discuss it. A naive position. And how could I starve to death in two days, particularly having recently lunched upon oxtail soup. People last for weeks so long as water is available.

Why am I against action. I was late to sign-on this morning though prepared for hours beforehand. Waken early these days or sometimes late. If I had ten pence I would enter super-markets and steal flat items. And talking about water I can make tea, one cup of which gives the idea if not the sustenance of soup because of the tea bag's encrustation viz crumbs of old food, oose, hair, dandruff and dust. Maybe the new girl shall come borrow sugar from me. And then what will transpire. If

Had to go for a slash there and action: the thing being held between middle finger and thumb with the index slightly bent at the first joint so that the outside, including the nail, lay along it; a pleasant, natural grip. If I had held the index a fraction more bent I would have soaked the linoleum to the side of the pot. And the crux is of course that the act is natural. I have never set out to pish in that manner. It simply happens. Everyman the same I suppose with minute adjustments here and there according to differing chopper measurements. Yet surely the length of finger will vary in relation. Logical thought at last. Coherence is attainable as far as the learned Hamish Smith of Esher Suffolk would have us believe. I am no Englishman. I am for nationalization on a national scale and if you are a smalltrader well

No point journeying forth before opening time.

It is possible I might eat with the neighbours as a last resort and perhaps watch television although in view of the oxtail soup a deal to hope for. But I would far rather be abroad in a tavern in earnest conversation with keen people over the state of nations, and I vow to listen. No day dreaming or vacant gazing right hand up and honest to god. Nor shall I inadvertently yawn hugely. But my condition is such company is imperative. I can no longer remain with myself. And that includes Percy, Greta and the infant, let us say Gloria — all three of whom I shall term the Nulties. The Nulties are a brave little unit gallantly making their way through a harsh uncaring world. They married in late life and having endeavoured for a little one were overwhelmed by their success. The infant Gloria is considered not a bad looking child though personally her looks dont appeal. She has a very tiny nose, pointed ears, receding hair. Also she shits over everything. Mainly diarrhoea that has an amazingly syrupy smell. Like many mothers Greta doesnt always realise the smell exists while on the other hand is absolutely aware so that she begins apologising left right and centre. Yet if everybody resembles me no wonder she forgets the bastarn smell because I for the sake of decency am liable to reply: What smell?

Greta is a busy mum with scarce the time for outside interests. There is nothing or perhaps a lot to say about Percy but it is hell of a boring. The point is that one of these days he shall awaken to an empty house. The woman will have upped and gone and with any sense will have neglected to uplift the infant. Trouble with many mothers is their falling for the propaganda dished out concerning them ie. and their offspring — Woman's Own magazines and that kind of shite. Most men fall for it too. But I am being sidetracked by gibberish. No, I fail to fit into their cosy scene for various reasons the most obvious of which is 3's a crowd and that's that for the time being.

But dear god I cannot eat with them tonight. They skimp on grub. One Saturday (and the straits must have been beyond desperation if Saturday it truly was) they sat me down and we set to on a plate of toast and tinned spaghetti. For the evening repast! My christ. But what I said was, Toast and spaghetti, great stuff. Now how can I tell such untruths and is it any wonder that I'm fucking languishing. No, definitely not. I deserve all of it. Imitation tomato sauce on my chin. And after the meal we turn to the telly over a digestive smoke and pitcher of coffee essence & recently boiled water; and gape our way to the Late Weather. I could make the poor old Nulties even worse by saying they stand for God Save The Queen Of The Great English Speakers but they dont to my knowledge — it is possible they wait till I have departed upstairs.

I have no wish to continue a life of the Nulties.

Something must be done. A decisive course of action. Tramping around pubs in the offchance of bumping into wealthy acquaintances is a depressing affair. And as far as I remember none of mine are wealthy and even then it is never a doddle to beg from acquaintances — hard enough with friends. Of which I no longer have. No fucking wonder. But old friends I no longer see can no longer be termed friends and since they are obliged to be something I describe them as acquaintances. In fact every last individual I recollect at a given moment is logically entitled to be termed acquaintance. And yet

Why the lies. concerning the tapping of a few bob; I find it easy. Never in the least embarrassed though occasionally I have recourse to the expression of such in order to be adduced ethical or something. I am a natural born beggar. Yes. Honest. A natural born beggar. I should take permanently to the road.

The pubs I tramp are those used by former colleagues, fellow employees of the many firms which have in the past employed me for mutual profit. My christ. Only when skint and totally out of the game do I consider the tramp. Yet apparently my company is not anathema. Eccentric but not unlikeable. A healthy respect is perhaps accorded one. Untrue. I am treated in the manner of a sick younger brother. It is my absolute lack of interest in any subject that may arise in their conversation that appeals to them. I dislike debates, confessions and New Year resolutions. I answer only in monosyllables, even when women are present: Still Waters Run Deep is the adage I expect them to use of me. But there are no grounds for complaint. Neither from them nor from me. All I ask is the free bevy, the smoke, the heat. It could embarrass somebody less sensitive than myself. What was that. No, there are weightier problems. The bathwater has been running. Is the new girl about to dip a daintily naked toe. Maybe it is Mrs. Soinson. Or Greta. And the infant Gloria. And Percy by christ. But no, Percy showers in the work to save the ten pence meter money. Petty petty petty. I dont bathe at all. I have what might be described as an allover-bodywash here in the kitchenette sink. I do every part of my surface bar certain sections of my lower to middle back which are impossible to reach without one of those long stemmed brushes I often saw years ago in amazing American Movies.

Incredible. Someone decides to bathe in a bath and so the rest of us are forced to run the risk of bladder infection. Nobody chapped my door. How do they know I didnt need to go. So inconsiderate for fuck sake that's really bad. Too much tea right enough, that's the problem.

No, Greta probably entertains no thoughts at all of being in bed with me. I once contemplated the possibility of Percy entertaining such notions. But I must immediately confess to this strong dislike as mutual. And he is most unattractive. And whereas almost any woman is attractive and desirable only a slender few men are. I dont of course mean slenderly proportioned men, in fact — what is this at all. I dont want to sleep with men right hand up and honest to god I dont. Why such strenuous denials my good fellow. No reason. Oho. Honest. Okay then. It's a meal I need, a few pints, a smoke, open air and outlook, the secure abode. Concerted energy, decisive course of action. Satisfyingly gainful employment. Money. A decidable and complete system of life. Ungibberishness. So many needs and the nonexistent funds. I must leave these square quarters of mine this very night. I must worm my way into company, any company, and the more ingratiatingly the better.

Having dug out a pair of uncracked socks I have often made the normal ablutions and left these quarters with or without the Imitation Crombie. Beginning in a pub near the city centre I find nobody. Now to start a quest such as this in a fashion such as this is fucking awful. Not uncommon nevertheless yet this same pub is always the first pub and must always be the first pub in this the quest.

Utter rubbish. How in the name of christ can one possibly consider suicide when one's giro arrives in two days' time. Two days. But it is still Thursday. Thursday. Surely midnight has passed and so technically it is tomorrow morning, the next day — Friday. Friday morning. O jesus and tomorrow the world. Amen. Giro tomorrow. In a bad way, no. Certainly not. Who are you kidding. I have to sleep. Tomorrow ie. tonight is Friday's sleep. But two sleeps equal two days. What am I facing here. And so what. I wish

To hell with that for a game.

But I did move recently. I sought out my fellows. Did I really though. As a crux this could be imperative, analogous to the deathwish. Even considering the possibility sheds doubt. Not necessarily. In fact I dont believe it for a single solitary minute. I did want to get in with a crowd though, surely to christ. Maybe

I wasnt trying hard enough. But I honestly required company. Perhaps they had altered their drinking habits. Because of me. In the name of fuck all they had to do was humiliate me—not that I would have been bothered by it but at least it could have allayed their feelings — as if some sort of showdown had taken place. But to actually change their pub. Well well well. Perhaps they sense I was setting out on a tramp and remained indoors with shutters drawn, lights extinguished. My christ I'm predictable. Three pubs I went to and I gave up. Always been the same: I lack follow through. Ach.

Can I really say I enjoy life with money. When I have it I throw it away. Only relax when skint. When skint I am a hulk — husk. No sidesteps from the issue. I do not want money ergo I do not want to be happy. The current me is my heart's desire. Surely not. Yet it appears the case. I am always needing money and I am always getting rid of it. This must be hammered home to me. Not even a question of wrecking my life, just that I am content to wallow. Nay, enjoy. I should commit suicide. Unconsecrated ground shall be my eternal resting spot. But why commit suicide if enjoying oneself. Come out of hiding Hamish Smith. Esher Suffolk cannot hold you.

Next time the landlord shows up I shall drygulch him; stab him to death and steal his lot. Stab him to death. Sick to the teeth of day dreams. As if I could stab the nyaff. Maybe I could pick a fight with him and smash in his skull with a broken wine bottle and crash, blood and brains and wine over my wrist and clenched fist. The deathwish after all. Albeit murder. Sounds more rational that: ie. why destroy one's own life if enjoyable. No reason at all. Is there a question. None whatsoever, in fact I might be onto something deep here but too late to pursue it, too late. Yet it could be a revelation of an extraordinary nature. But previously of course been exhausted by the learned Smith of Esher decades since and nowadays taken for granted — not even a topic on an inferior year's O-level examination paper.

He isnt even a landlord. I refer to him as such but in reality he is only the bastarn agent. I dont know who the actual landlord really is. It might be Winsom Properties. Winsom Properties is a trust. That means you never know who you are dealing with. I dont like this kind of carry on. I prefer to know names.

Hell with them and their fucking shutters and lights out.

It isnt as bad as all that; here I am and it is now the short a.m.'s. The short a.m.'s. I await the water boiling for a final cup of tea. Probably only drink the stuff in order to pish. Does offer a sort of relief. And simply strolling to the kitchenette and preparing this tea: the gushing tap, the kettle, gathering the tea-bag from the crumb strewn shelf — all of this is motion.

My head gets thick.

One of the chief characteristics of my early, mid and late adolescence was the catastrophic form of the erotic content. Catastrophic in the sense that that which I did have was totally, well, not quite, fantasy. And is the lack by implication of an unnatural variety. Whether it is something to do with me or not — I mean whether or not it is catastrophic is nothing to do with me I mean, not at all. No.

Mr Smith, where are you. No, I cannot be bothered considering the early years. Who cares. Me of course it was fucking lousy. I masturbated frequently. My imagination was/is such I always had fresh stores of fantasies. And I dont wish to give the impression I still masturbate; nowadays, for example, I encounter difficulties in sustaining an erection unless another person happens to be in the immediate vicinity. Even first thing in the morning. This is all bastarn lies. Why in the name of fuck do I continue. What is it with me at all. Something must have upset me recently. Erotic content by christ. Why am I wiped out. Utterly skint. Eh. Why is this always as usual. Why do I even

Certain clerks behind the counter.

I mend fuses for people, oddjobs and that kind of bla for associates of the nyaff, tenants in other words. I am expected to do it. I allow my — I fall behind with the fucking rent. Terrible situation. I have to keep on his right side. Anyway, I dont mind the oddjobs. It gets you out and about.

I used to give him openings for a life of Mrs Soinson but all he could ever manage was, Fussy Old Biddy. And neither he nor she is married. I cant figure the woman out myself. Apart from her I might be the longest tenant on the premises. And when the nyaff knows so little about her you can be sure nobody else knows a thing. She must mend her own fuses. I havent even seen inside her room or rooms. It is highly possible that she actually fails to see me when we pass on the staircase. The nyaff regards her in awe. Is she a blacksheep outcast of an influential family closely connected to Winsom Properties. When he first became agent around here I think he looked upon her as easy meat whatever the hell that might mean as far as a nyaff is concerned. And she cant be more than fifty years of age, carries herself well and would seem an obvious widow. But I dispute that. A man probably wronged her many years ago. Jilted. With her beautiful 16 year old younger sister by her as bridesmaid, an engagement ring on her finger just decorously biding her time till this marriage of her big sister is out the way so she can step in and get married to her own youthful admirer, and on the other side of poor old Mrs Soinson stood her widowed father or should I say sat since he would have been an invalid and in his carriage, only waiting his eldest daughter's marriage so he can join his dearly departed who died in childbirth (that of the beautiful 16 year old) up there in heaven. And ever since that day Mrs Soinson has remained a spinster, virginal, the dutiful but pathetic aunt — a role she hates but accepts for her parents' memory. Or she could have looked after the aged father till it was too late and for some reason, on the day he died, vowed to stay a single lassie since nobody could take the place of the departed dad and took on the title of Mistress to ward off would-be suitors although of course you do find men more willing to entertain a single Mrs as opposed to a single Miss which is why I agree with Womens Lib. Ms should be the title of both married and single women.

In the name of god.

Taking everything into consideration the time may be approaching when I shall begin regularly paid, full-time employment. My lot is severely trying. For an approximate age I have been receiving money from the state. I am obliged to cease this malingering and earn an honest penny. Having lived in this fashion for so long I am well nigh unemployable and if I were an Industrial Magnate or Captain of Industry I would certainly entertain doubts as to my capacity for toil. I am an idle goodfornothing. A neerdowell. The workhouse is too good for the likes of me. I own up. I am incompatible with this Great British Society. My production rate is less than atrocious. An honest labouring job is outwith my grasp. Wielding a shabby brush is not to be my lot. Never more shall I be setting forth on bitter mornings just at the break of dawn through slimy backstreet alleys, the treacherous urban undergrowth, trudging the meanest cobbled streets and hideously misshapen pathways of this grey with a heart of gold city. Where is that godforsaken factory. Let me at it. A trier. I would say so Your Magnateship. And was Never Say Die the type of adage one could apply to the wretch. I believe so Your Industrialness.

Fuck off.

Often I sit by the window in order to sort myself out — a group therapy within, and I am content with a behaviourist approach, none of that pie-in-the-sky metaphysics here if you dont mind. I quick-fire trip questions at myself which demand immediate answers and sometimes elongated thought out ones. So far I have been unsuccessful, and the most honest comment on this is that it is done unintentionally on purpose, a very deeply structured item. Choosing this window for instance only reinforces the point. I am way way on top, high above the street. And though the outlook is unopen considerable activity takes place directly below. In future I may dabble in psychiatry — get a book out the library on the subject and stick in, go to nightschool and obtain the necessary qualifications for minor university acceptance whose exams I shall scrape through, industrious but lacking the spark of genius, and eventually make it into a general sanatorium leading a life of devotion to the mental health of mankind. I would really enjoy the work. I would like to organise beneficial group therapies and the rest of it. Daily discussions. Saving young men and women from all kinds of breakdowns. And you would definitely have to be alert working beside the average headbanger or disturbed soul who are in reality the sane and we the insane according to the learned H. S. of Esher S. But though I appear to jest I give plenty thought to the subject. At least once during their days everybody has considered themselves mad or at least well on the road but fortunately from listening to the BBC they realise that if they really were mad they would never for one moment consider it as a possible description of their condition although sometimes they almost have to when reading a book by an enlightened foreigner or watching a heavy play or documentary or something — I mean later, when lying in bed with the lights out for example with the wife fast asleep and $8\frac{1}{2}$ months pregnant maybe then suddenly he advances and not too accidentally bumps her on the shoulder all ready with some shite about, O sorry if I disturbed you, tossing and turning etc but I was just wondering eh . . . And then it dawns on him, this, the awful truth, he is off his head or at best has an astonishingly bad memory — and this memory, under the circumstances may actually be at worst. And that enlightened foreigner is no comfort once she will have returned to slumber and you are on your own, alone, in the middle of the night, the dark recesses and so on dan d ran dan. But it must happen sometimes. What must fucking happen.

The postoffice may be seeking reliable men. Perhaps I shall fail their medical. And that goes for the fireservice. But the armed forces. Security. And each branch is willing and eager to take on such as myself. I shall apply. The Military Life would suit me. Uplift the responsibility, the decision making, temptations, choices. And a sound bank account at the wind up — not a vast sum of course but enough to set me up as a tobacconist cum newsagent in a small way, nothing fancy, just to eke out the pension.

But there should be direction at 30 years of age. A knowing where I am going. Alright Sir Hamish we cant all be Charles Clore and Florence Nightingale but at least we damn well have a go and dont give in. Okay we may realise what it is all about and to hell with their christianity, ethics, the whole shebang and advertising but do we give in, do we Give Up The Ghost. No sirree by god we dont. Do you for one moment think we believe someone should starve to death while another feeds his dog on the finest fillet of steak and chips. Of course not. We none of us have outmoded beliefs but do we

I cannot place a finger somewhere. The bastarn rain is the cause. It pours, steadily for a time then heavier. Of course the fucking gutter has rotted and the constant torrent drops just above the fucking window. That bastard of a landlord gets nothing done, too busy peeping through keyholes at poor old Mrs Soinson. I am fed up with it. Weather been terrible for years. No wonder people look the way they do. Who can blame them. Christ it is bad, the weather, so fucking consistent. Depresses everything. Recently I went for a short jaunt in the disagreeable countryside. Fortunately I got soaked through. The cattle ignored the rain. The few motor cars around splished past squirting oily mud onto the Imitation Crombie. I kept slipping into marshy bogs from whence I shrieked at various objects while seated. It wasnt boring. Of yore, on country rambles, I would doze in some deserted field with the sun beating etc the hum of grasshoppers chirp. I never sleep in a field where cattle graze lest I get nibbled. The countryside and I are incompatible. Everybody maintains they like the countryside but I refuse to accept such nonsense. It is absurd. Just scared, to admit the truth — that they hate even the idea of journeying through pastureland or craggyland. Jesus christ. I dont mind small streams burning through arable-land. Hardy fishermen with waders knee-deep in lonely inshore waters earn my total indifference. Not exactly. Not sympathy either, nor pity, nor respect, envy, hate. Contempt. No, not at all. But I heroworship lighthousekeepers. No. Envy is closer. Or maybe jealousy. And anyway, nowadays all men are created equal. But whenever I have had money in the past I always enjoyed the downpour. If on the road to somewhere the rain is fine. A set purpose. Even the cinema. Coat collar upturned, street lights reflecting on puddles, arriving with wind flushed complexion and rubbing your damp hands, parking your arse on a convenient convector heater. But without the money. Still not too bad perhaps.

According to the mirror I have been going about with a thoughtful expression on one's countenance. I appear to have become aware of myself in relation to the field by which I mean the external world. In relation to this field I am in full knowledge of my position. And this has nothing to do with steak & chips

Comfortable degrees of security are not to be scoffed at. I doff the cap to those who attain it the bastards. Seriously, I am fed up with being fed up. What I do wish

I shall not entertain day dreams
I shall not fantasise
I shall endeavour to make things work

I shall tramp the mean streets in search of menial posts or skilled ones. Everywhere I shall go, from Shetland Oilrigs to Bearsden Gardening Jobs. To Gloucestershire even. I would go to Gloucestershire. Would I fuck. To hell with them and their cricket & cheese. I refuse to go there. I may emigrate to The Great Englishes — o jesus christ Australia & New Zealand. Or America and Canada.

All I'm fucking asking is regular giros and punctual counter clerks.

Ach well son cheer up. So quiet in this dump. Some kind of tune was droning around a while back. I was sitting clapping hands to the rhythm and considering moving about on the floor. I used to dream of playing the banjo. Or even the guitar, just being able to strum but with a passable voice I could be dropping into parties and playing a song, couple of women at the feet keeping time and slowly sipping from a tall glass, 4 in the a.m.'s with whisky on the shelf and plenty of smokes. This is it now. Definitely.

black and white consumer and producer parasite thief come on shake hands you lot

Well throw yourself out the fucking window then. Throw myself out fuck all window — do what you like but here I am, no suicide and no malnutrition, no fucking nothing in fact because I am leaving, I am getting to fuck out of it. A temporary highly paid job, save a right few quid and then off on one's travels. Things will be done. Action immediate. Of the Pioneering Stock would you say. Of that ilk most certainly Your Worship. And were the audience Clambering to their Feet. I should think so Your Grace.

The fact is I am a late starter. I am

I shouldnt be bothering about money anyway. The creditors have probably forgotten all about my existence. No point worrying about other than current arrears. The old me wouldnt require funds. A red & white polkadot handkerchief, a stout sapling rod, the hearty whistle and hi yo silver for the short ride to the outskirts of town, Carlisle and points south.

It is all a load of shite. I often plan things out then before the last minute do something ridiculous to ensure the plan's failure. If I did decide to clear the arrears and get a few quid together, follow up with a symbolic burning of the Imitation Crombie and in short make preparations to mend my ways I could conceivably enlist in the Majestic Navy to spite myself — or even fork out a couple of month's rent in advance for this dump simply to sit back and enjoy my next step from a safe distance and all the time guffawing in the background good christ I am schizophrenic, I never thought I acted in that manner yet I must admit it sounds like me, worse than I imagined, bad, bad. Maybe I could use the cash to pay for an extended stay in a private nursing home geared to the needs of the Unabletocope. But can it be schizophrenia if I can identify it myself. Doubtful. However, I regard

I was of the opinion certain items in regard to my future had been resolved. Cynical of self, this is the problem. Each time I make a firm resolution I end up scoffing. Yes. I sneer. Well well well, what a shite. That really does take the biscuit. And look at the time look at the time.

Captains of Industry should create situations for my ilk. The Works Philosopher I could be. With my own wee room to the left of the Personnel Section. During teabreaks Dissidents would be sent to me. Militancy could be cut by half, maybe as much as 90%. Yet Works Philosophers could not be classed as staff, instead they would be stamping in & out like the rest of the troops just in case they get aspirations, and seek reclassification within Personnel maybe. Gibberish. And yet fine, that would be fine, so what if they got onto the staff because that would leave space for others and the Dissident next in line could become the new Works Philosopher and so on and so forth. And they would stick it, the job, they would not be obliged to seek out square squarters whose shelves are crumb strewn.

I shall have it to grips soon. Tomorrow or who knows. After all, I am but 30, hardly matured. But fuck me I'm getting hell of a hairy these days. Maybe visit the barber in the near future, Saturday morning for instance, who knows what is in store. Only waiting for my passion to find an object and let itself go. Yes, who can tell what's in store, that's the great thing about life, always one more fish in the sea, iron in the fire; this is the great thing about life, the uncertainty and the bla

Jesus what will I do, save up for a new life, the mending of the ways, pay off arrears, knock the door of accredited creditors, yes, I can still decide what to do about things concerning myself and even others if only in regard to me at least it is still indirectly to do with them and yet it isnt indirect at all because it is logically bound to be direct if it is anything and obviously it is something and must therefore be directly since I am involved and if they are well

well well, who can tell what the fuck this is about. I am chucking it in. My brain cannot cope on its own. Gets carried away for the sake of thought no matter whether it be sense or not, no, that is the last fucking thing considered. Which presents problems. I really do have a hard time knowing where I am going. For if going, where. Nowhere or somewhere. Children and hot meals. Homes and security and the neighbours in for a quiet drink at the weekend. Tumbling on carpets with the weans and television sets and golf and even heated discussions in jocular mood while the wives gossip ben in the kitchen and   —

Now then: here I am in curiously meagre surroundings, living the life of a hapless pauper, my pieces of miserable silver supplied gratis by the Browbeaten Taxpayer. The past ramblings concerning outer change were pure invention. And comments made about one's total inadequacy were done so in earnest albeit with a touch of pride. Even the brave Nulties are abused by me, at least in respect to grub & smokes. And all for what. Ah, an ugly sight. But this must be admitted: with a rumbling stomach I have often refused food, preferring a lonely smoke and the possible mystery of, Has he eaten elsewhere . . . and if so with whom. Yet for all people know I have several trunks packed full of articles, clothes and whatnot. Apart from a couple of clerks nobody knows a thing about me. I could be a Man about Town. They probably nudge each other and refer to me as a bit of a lad. I might start humping large suitcases plastered with illegible labels. Save up and buy a suit in modern mode. Get my coat dyed, even stick with its symbolic burning. Or else I could sell it. A shrewd man I occasionally have dealings with rejected this coat. But I did ask a Big price. Shoes too I need. Presently I have what are described as Bumpers. Whereas with real leather efforts and a new rig out I could travel anywhere and get a new start in life. I could be a Computer Programmer. But they're supposed to reach their peak at 21 years of age. Still and all the sex potency fucking peak is 16. 16 years of age by christ you could not credit that. Ach. I dare say sex plays more of a role in my life than grub. If both were in abundance my problems could only increase. Yet one's mental capacities would be bound to make more use of their potential without problems at the fundamental level.

But

the plan. From now on I do not cash giros. I sleep in on Saturday mornings and so too late for the postoffice until Monday mornings by which time everything will be alright, it will be fine, I shall have it worked out and fine and if I can stretch it out and grab at next Saturday then the pathway shall have been erected, I shall have won through.

Recently I lived in seclusion. For a considerable period I existed on a tiny islet not far from Toay. Sheep and swooping gulls for companions. The land and the sea. After dark the inner recesses. Self knowledge and acceptance of the awareness. No trees of course. None. Sheer drops from mountainous regions, bird shit and that of sheep and goats as well perhaps, in that kind of terrain. No sign of man or woman. The sun always far in the sky but no clouds. Not tanned either. Weatherbeaten. Hair matted by the salt spray. Food requires no mention. Swirling eddies within the standing rocks and nicotine wool stuck to the jaggy edges, the droppings of the gulls.

Since I shall have nothing to look forwards to on Saturday mornings I must reach a state of neither up nor down. Always the same. That will be miserable I presume but considering my heart's desire is to be miserable then with uncashed giros reaching for the ceiling I can be indefinitely miserable. Total misery. However, to retain misery I may be obliged to get out and about in order not to be always miserable since — or should I say pleasure is imperative if perfect misery is the goal; and, therefore, a basic condition of my perpetual misery is the occasional jaunt abroad in quest of joy. Now we're getting somewhere Sir Smith, arise and get your purple sash. And since ambling round pubs only depresses me I must seek out other means of entertainment or henceforth desist this description of myself as wretch. And setbacks and kicksintheteeth are out of the question. Masochism then. Is this what

Obviously I am just in the middle of a nervous breakdown, even saying it I mean that alone

But for christ sake saving a year's uncashed giros is impossible because the bastards render them uncashable after a 6 month interval.

Walking from Land's End to John O'Groats would be ideal in fact because for one thing it would tax my resistance to the utmost. Slogging on day in day out. Have to be during the summer. I dislike the cold water and I would be stopping off for a swim. Yet this not knowing how long it takes the average walker . . . well, why worry, time is of no concern. Or perhaps it should be. I could try for the record. After the second attempt possibly. Once I had my bearings. Not at all. I would amble. And with pendants and flags attached to the suitcase I could beg my grub & tobacco. The minimum money required. Neither broo nor social security. The self sufficiency of the sweetly self employed. I could be for the rest of my life. The Land's End to John O'Groats man. That would be my title. My name a byword, although anonymity would be the thing to aim for. Jesus it could be good. And far from impossible. I have often hitched about the place. Many times. But hitching must be banned otherwise I shall be saving time which is of course an absurdity — pointless to hitch. And yet what difference will it make if I do save time because it can make no difference anyway. None whatsoever. Not at all. And if it takes 6 weeks a trip and the same back up I could average 4 return trips a year. If I am halfway through life just now ie. a hundred and twenty return trips then in another hundred and twenty trips I would be dead. I can mark off each trip on milestones north & south. And when the media get a grip of me I can simply say I'll be calling a halt in 80 trips time. And I speak of returns. That would be twenty years hence by which time I would have become accustomed to fame. Although I could have fallen down dead by then through fatigue or something. Hail rain shine. The dead of winter would be a challenge and could force me into shelter unless I acquire a passport and head out to sunnier climes, Australia for example to stave off the language barriers yet speech need be no problem since communication will be the major lack as intention perhaps. No, impossible. I cannot leave The Great British Shores. Comes to that I cannot leave the Scottish ones either. Yes, aye, Scotland is ideal. Straight round the Scottish Coast from the foot of Galloway right round to Berwick although Ayrshire is a worry its being a very boring coastline. But boredom is out of the question. Ayrshire will not be denied. So each return trip might involve say a four month slog if keeping rigidly to the coast on all minor roads particularly when you consider Kintyre — or Morven by fuck and even I suppose Galloway itself to some extent. But that kind of thing is easily resolved. I dont have to restrict myself to mapped out routes from which the slightest deviation is frowned upon. On the contrary, that last minute decision at the country crossroads can only enhance the affair. And certain items of clothing are already marked out as essential items. The stout boots and gnarled staff to ward off country animals after dusk. A hat & coat for wet weather. The Imitation Crombie may suffice. Though an anorak to cover the knees would probably reap dividends. And after a few return trips — and being a circular route no such thing as a return would exist ie. I would be travelling on an arc — the farmfolk and country dwellers would know me well, the goodwives leaving thick winter woollies by the side of the road, flasks of oxtail soup under hedges. Shepherds offering shelter in remote bothies by the blazing log fires sipping hot toddies for the wildest nights and plenty of tobacco always the one essential luxury, and the children up and down the land crying, Mummy here comes the Scottish Coastroad Walker while I would dispense the homespun philosophies of the daisy growing and the planet as it revolves etc. A stray dog joining me having tagged along for a trip at a safe distance behind me I at last turn and at my first grunt of encouragement it comes bounding joyfully forwards to shower me in wet noses and barked assurances to stick by me through thick & thin and to eternally guard my last lowly grave when I have at length fallen in midstride plumb tuckered out after many years viz 12 round trips at two years a trip. Yet it might be shorter than that. While the hot days in central summer are the busloads of tourists arriving to see me, pointed out by their driver, the Legend of the North, the solitary trudging humpbacked figure with dog & gnarled staff just vanishing out of sight into the mist, Dont give him money Your Lordship you'll just hurt his feelings. Just a bit of your cheese piece and a saucer of milk for the whelp. Group photographs with me peering suspiciously at the camera from behind shoulders at the back or in the immediate foreground perhaps, It is rumoured the man was a Captain of Industry Your Grace, been right round the Scottish Coastroad 28 times and known from Galloway to Berwick as a friend to Everyone. Yes, just a pinch of your snuff and a packet of cigarette-papers for chewing purposes only. No sextants or compasses or any of that kind of shite but

A Selected List of Titles Available from Minerva

While every effort is made to keep prices low, it is sometimes necessary to increase prices at short notice. Mandarin Paperbacks reserves the right to show new retail prices on covers which may differ from those previously advertised in the text or elsewhere.

The prices shown below were correct at the time of going to press.

Fiction

☐	7493 9026 3	**I Pass Like Night**	Jonathan Ames	£3.99	BX
☐	7493 9006 9	**The Tidewater Tales**	John Bath	£4.99	BX
☐	7493 9004 2	**A Casual Brutality**	Neil Blessondath	£4.50	BX
☐	7493 9028 2	**Interior**	Justin Cartwright	£3.99	BC
☐	7493 9002 6	**No Telephone to Heaven**	Michelle Cliff	£3.99	BX
☐	7493 9028 X	**Not Not While the Giro**	James Kelman	£4.50	BX
☐	7493 9011 5	**Parable of the Blind**	Gert Hofmann	£3.99	BC
☐	7493 9010 7	**The Inventor**	Jakov Lind	£3.99	BC
☐	7493 9003 4	**Fall of the Imam**	Nawal El Saadewi	£3.99	BC

Non-Fiction

☐	7493 9012 3	**Days in the Life**	Jonathon Green	£4.99	BC
☐	7493 9019 0	**In Search of J D Salinger**	Ian Hamilton	£4.99	BX
☐	7493 9023 9	**Stealing from a Deep Place**	Brian Hall	£3.99	BX
☐	7493 9005 0	**The Orton Diaries**	John Lahr	£5.99	BC
☐	7493 9014 X	**Nora**	Brenda Maddox	£6.99	BC

All these books are available at your bookshop or newsagent, or can be ordered direct from the publisher. Just tick the titles you want and fill in the form below. Available in:
BX: British Commonwealth excluding Canada
BC: British Commonwealth including Canada

Mandarin Paperbacks, Cash Sales Department, PO Box 11, Falmouth, Cornwall TR10 9EN.

Please send cheque or postal order, no currency, for purchase price quoted and allow the following for postage and packing:

UK	80p for the first book, 20p for each additional book ordered to a maximum charge of £2.00.
BFPO	80p for the first book, 20p for each additional book.
Overseas including Eire	£1.50 for the first book, £1.00 for the second and 30p for each additional book thereafter.

NAME (Block letters) ....

ADDRESS ....

....

....